LINC

me

K mommy

Horatio

My New Family

Please address questions and book requests to: Silhouette Reader Service
U.S.: 3010 Walden Ave., P.O. Box 1325, Buffalo, NY 14269
Canadian: P.O. Box 609, Fort Erie, Ont. L2A 5X3

# Born in the USA

## UTAH

# Pat Tracy

## Wild Streak

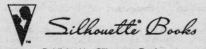

Silhouette Books

Published by Silhouette Books

**America's Publisher of Contemporary Romance**

**SILHOUETTE BOOKS**
300 East 42nd St.,
New York, N.Y. 10017

ISBN 0-373-47194-7

WILD STREAK

Dear Reader,

I chose Salt Lake City, Utah, as the setting for Erin and Linc's story because I once lived there and was impressed by the warm, Western hospitality extended to newcomers. The rugged Wasatch mountains rise above a beautiful, lush valley that, with backbreaking toil, early pioneers wrestled from a desert wasteland. The Salt Lake Valley is a testament to America's pioneer spirit and the willingness of its people to come together for a great cause.

For Erin and Linc to claim the love fate has denied them requires the same courage it takes to tame a wild land. I believe those hearty settlers were blessed with both endurance and *humor*. Our ability to laugh in the midst of uncertainty lifts our spirits and cocoons wounded hearts in rainbows of hope.

A rainbow for every heart…I'm grateful a loving Heavenly Father has made it so.

Warmest regards,

Pat Tracy

# Chapter One

Short and sweet, that's how he would handle tonight's showdown with Erin. He would tell her the way things were going to be and she would accept them—simple as that. Linc shut off the idling engine of his rental car and leaned over the steering wheel.

Dusk enveloped the Salt Lake City, Utah, neighborhood, creating the illusion that Linc was once again imagining his surroundings—as he had imagined them so often during the past year.

Across the wide, tree-lined street a stately two-story, white brick home held his attention as he opened the car door and stepped out. The pavement beneath him was real, as real as the scents of freshly cut grass and pine shrubbery. The thought of seeing Erin again made Linc's skin prickle with a tremor of edgy expectation. How had he tolerated the past twelve months of his self-inflicted banishment from her life?

A year ago Linc had accepted that banishment as the restitution demanded of him for lusting after his best friend's wife. Tonight Linc was ready to declare the price paid. He was tired of living with guilt, the kind of guilt that could burrow under a man's skin—a man's resolve—and push him over the edge.

He squared his shoulders and moved forward. Linc knew beyond a shadow of a doubt that if their corporate attorney hadn't ordered him to put in an appearance at next week's board meeting, he would still be in Los Angeles. His jaw tightened. He had every intention of settling matters with Erin tonight. Once he straightened her out, there would be no need for Wednesday's board meeting, and Linc could be on his way back to California.

As he crossed the street, it soothed Linc's ragged sense of control to think of tonight's confrontation as the shoring up of a structure that had already proven itself strong enough to withstand the most violent of storms.

Very soon he would prove to himself that the woman who had haunted him for a year of lonely nights was a ghost he'd finally exorcised.

"Isn't it nice that we're adults, Erin?"

Erin glanced across the car's interior at her date. Paul wore an expression of complacency. "That's something I tend to take for granted," she answered noncommittally.

He stretched his arm along the back of the seat. "Well, think about it," he prompted, inching closer. "We're both consenting adults. There's nothing stopping us from going inside and...letting nature take its course.''

Erin was stunned by her mild-mannered accountant's words, and her fingers closed on the car's door handle. She was grateful that Paul had decided to have this conversation in her driveway. ''Since this is our first date, I hardly think—''

''Don't think,'' he interrupted with a sly smile. ''Let biology take over. You've been a widow for more than a year, Erin. You're a young, vibrant woman with...needs.'' His hand drifted to her shoulder. ''I'm more than willing to take care of those needs for you—with no strings attached, of course.''

Quickly Erin opened the car door and stepped into the autumn night. Her decision to start dating again no longer seemed as good an idea as it had last week when she'd accepted Paul's dinner invitation.

Briskly, she leaned forward. ''Goodbye, Paul.''

Before he could reply, she straightened and closed the door with finality.

The sound of leaves crunching underfoot accompanied her to the front porch. She was struggling to extract the house key from her purse when Paul joined her on the step. ''Hey, wait a minute.''

She paused, but already her thoughts were focused upon her young son. Had Joshua drifted off to sleep peaceably for Kristi, or had he put up a struggle?

Paul edged closer. ''I hope you didn't take what I said the wrong way.''

Frowning, Erin faced him. ''It's late, Paul.''

''So, I come alive after midnight, honey.''

*Just like shower mildew...* ''I have no intention of—''

He reached out and fingered the lace at her throat. "I think a kiss is definitely in order."

Erin's jaw went slack. Never in a million years would she have expected tonight's date to end with Paul making a pass at her. "Listen here, I—"

Her front door swung open, and a towering male form filled the doorway. Abruptly recognition slapped Erin in the face. A squeak of surprise died in her throat.

Linc was back.

"The lady said no, sleaze ball. It's time to pack it in."

Barely conscious of Paul's hasty departure, Erin gazed numbly at Linc Severance. In the porch light, disapproval tightened his leanly sculpted face. Almost a year had passed since he'd walked out of her life, leaving her bereft of his compassion and support.

"Linc..." Saying his name aloud helped convince her that he was truly there.

His scowl darkened. "I'm surprised you haven't forgotten me."

Forgotten him... The anger and hurt and...*shame* she'd experienced a year ago when Linc's brother, Steve, had told her that Linc had gone back to Los Angeles returned full force. Erin clung to the anger—it empowered her.

She stepped past him and into her living room, not bothering to invite him inside. She suspected Linc would suit himself.

There was no sign of Kristi or her son. "Where—"

"I sent the sitter home," Linc said, closing the door behind him. "Joshua's in bed."

It infuriated Erin that Linc still had the knack of

reading her mind. She tossed her purse onto the couch and turned. It was important that she take control of the situation. Now was the time to demonstrate to Linc that the days of her being weak and ineffective were over.

"You had no right to send Kristi home."

His eyes narrowed. "That didn't stop me from doing it."

Erin grimaced. She should know better than to challenge the implacable Linc Severance. Though he was quiet-natured, she'd learned long ago that he reacted unpredictably to challenges.

She raised her chin. "Why?"

"Why did I send her home, or why did I come back?"

She refused to let the sudden intensity glittering in his dark eyes intimidate her. "Why not go for broke and answer both questions?"

"I sent Kristi home because there was no need for her to stay once I'd arrived. I asked her what she usually earned sitting for you, paid her twice that amount and sent her on her way."

"Alone? Into the night?" Erin demanded, incensed by his high-handed intrusion into her life.

Linc's lips thinned. "She lives next door."

"I know that," Erin snapped. "I wasn't sure you did."

"I've only been gone a year. I knew Kristi and she remembered me. Besides, I stood on the porch and watched her safely home," he returned evenly.

"So why are you here?" Erin asked, needing to know why Linc had suddenly reappeared in her life.

He shrugged. Resentfully she noticed the way his

gray suit followed the gesture, flattering his rangy frame. "My attorney didn't give me a choice."

He would insist on being vague. Well, two could play that game. "The rain in Spain stays mainly on the plain."

He didn't even blink. "So I've heard."

Erin stalked to the front door and opened it. "It was nice seeing you again, Linc."

"You can close the door, Erin," he said quietly. "I'm not going anywhere."

Erin prided herself on her even temper. She was a loving daughter, and an admirably patient mother to her four-year-old son. Even so, she could feel her cheeks heat with impatience.

She slammed the door shut. "I'm setting the ground rules, Linc." She took a step in his direction. "First, you don't come into my house unless you're invited. Second, you don't send home my baby-sitter. And third—"

"This isn't quite the homecoming I expected," he observed coolly.

"This isn't your home," she pointed out.

He slid his hands into his pockets. "All right, I'll admit I came on a little strong."

"That's big of you."

A muscle worked in his jaw. "There's no need for sarcasm, Erin."

Without warning, the pressure of hot tears built. Erin bowed her head, letting her hair shield her face. She would not let Linc see her cry.

The last time they'd been together she'd fallen asleep in his arms, crying. In the months following his departure, she'd assumed it had been her weakness that had driven him away. The memory of that weakness sent a rush of shame through her. Never again, she vowed. Never again would she betray any weakness or vulnerability before Linc Severance.

Calling upon a composure she hadn't known she possessed, Erin raised her head. "Sorry for the sarcasm." She drew a breath, wanting to ask him why he hadn't bothered saying goodbye before he'd left town last year. The words wouldn't be summoned past her tight throat. "So, how's life in Los Angeles?"

Brittle words to cover her brittle composure.

His eyes remained somber. "I had to leave, Erin. It was the right thing to do."

*The right thing to do!*

She stared at him numbly. How could he say that? Shakily she brushed a hand through her hair. At one time Linc had been her closest friend. She had shared her thoughts and feelings with him, thoughts and feelings Merrill never had the time or inclination to hear.

Had she asked too much of their friendship? Was that why Linc had turned from her, because she'd demanded too much of him?

When Merrill had died, she'd been selfish in her grief. Guilt could do that to a person, and she'd certainly felt guilty about being an instrument of her husband's death. During the emotionally chaotic weeks following Merrill's accident, Linc had become the rock from which she'd derived her strength. Last year when Linc had walked out of her life, he'd taken a hunk of that strength with him. He'd also taken her self-confidence and her trust.

If only Linc had told her she was becoming too

dependent—she would have understood and backed off. There was no need for him to sneak away like a thief into the night. She wouldn't have tried to hold him.

The urge to welcome him back, the urge to rest her head against his strong shoulder rose up suddenly. Determinedly Erin fought the weakness. She'd learned her lesson. Her days of leaning upon Linc Severance were behind her forever. "There's no fatted calf here, Linc. If that's what you expected, you've come to the wrong place."

He flinched. "Cheer up, Erin. Once we settle the matter of the dividends Prestige Builders is sending you each quarter, I'll be on a plane heading to L.A. and out of your life permanently."

His words were evenly paced, precise in a way that demonstrated as nothing else could have his indifference to the termination of the closeness they had once shared.

"I've already told you what you can do with those damned dividend checks."

His left eyebrow rose.

He didn't have to say anything for Erin to know what he was thinking. As a minister's daughter, she'd learned long ago that people took exception whenever she expressed herself too bluntly.

"I don't need your money," she whispered tightly. Another part of the legacy of being a minister's daughter was her aversion to anything resembling charity, especially now that she was an adult. Any kind of charity eroded her feelings of self-worth and hard-won independence. "Merrill's insurance is more than sufficient for Joshua and I to live on."

"And when it's time for Joshua to go to college?"

"That's my business."

Clearly exasperated, Linc shook his head. "You're being proud and foolish, Erin. If you would just be reasonable about this, there would be no need for a board meeting on Wednesday."

She balled her hands into fists. "Don't you get it? It's my life. Joshua and I will be fine. We don't need *anything* from Prestige Builders."

Linc stepped toward her.

She held her ground.

"You're the one who doesn't *get* it, Erin. Merrill was my best friend. I'm not going to stand by and watch his widow make a mess of his son's life. Joshua is entitled to those dividends."

Tears clouded her eyes. "We don't want or need your money."

"Mommy..."

It took a moment for the soft voice to penetrate the haze of Erin's anger. She whirled and saw Joshua ambling sleepily down the stairs. Visions of him tumbling to the bottom played in her mind, and her heart leaped in her chest.

"Joshua, wait, honey—"

Before the paralysis left her frozen limbs, Linc was already at the bottom of the staircase. When he picked up her son and held him briefly in his powerful arms, something painful gripped Erin's chest.

As she reached out to take Joshua's sleep-flushed body from Linc, she noticed her son's alarm at being held by a stranger. New pain knifed through her. A year ago, Joshua had known Linc and looked forward to his visits.

"I was thirsty, Mommy."

"I'll get you a drink, sweetheart."

She carried him into the kitchen and sat him on the counter next to her. He drank lazily, his eyelids falling closed, his drowsy body leaning against her. A wave of maternal love as strong as any emotion she'd ever experienced swept through her, and she rested her cheek against the silky swath of his dark hair.

When he had drunk his fill, she carried him upstairs, hoping perversely that Linc would offer to do it so she could turn him down. When Linc had walked out of her life, he'd abandoned her son, too. No amount of money could make up for that betrayal.

Guided by the muted glow of her son's night-light, she stepped into Joshua's bedroom. From the way he was relaxed against her, she knew he had fallen asleep again. Carefully she tucked him into bed, drawing the covers over his sprawled little body.

Her fingertips went to his forehead, and she brushed back a dark lock of hair. An aching tenderness welled inside her. She was looking at the most precious part of her life.

In sleep, Joshua looked soft and sweet and... vulnerable. No one would know what this past month of implementing her grand scheme to take control of her life had cost her emotionally. She was an overprotective mother and knew it. Still, because of the violent suddenness of Merrill's death and the insidious fear that she had contributed to it, she couldn't seem to help herself.

Noticing that Joshua's teddy bear had slipped to the floor, she stooped to retrieve it. Slowly, she ca-

ressed its worn fur. She had bought Ernest the afternoon she'd discovered she was pregnant.

The memories were poignant, haunting. Tears
formed. Not only had her son forgotten Linc, Joshua
had also forgotten his father. She wondered if she
should have done more to keep Merrill alive in her
young son's mind. She didn't know what she could
have done differently, but she felt as if she'd somehow failed Merrill—again. Pressing her face into Ernest's soft belly, she sent a silent prayer of apology
heavenward.

Sometimes she felt so inadequate to the task of
raising Joshua on her own. It didn't help her confidence to have Linc pop back into her life, bringing
up the subject of her son's college education—especially when her concerns were focused primarily on
the here and now.

What did she know of little boys? An image of
herself playing catch with an older version of Joshua
came to mind. It was a nice tableau of them together
at Wasatch Park on a beautiful spring day. But in her
heart, Erin knew there was more to raising a son than
tossing a ball to him.

*One day at a time, Erin. You take it one day at a
time.*

Linc's voice drifted into her troubled thoughts, providing an unexpected source of solace. In the days
following Merrill's death, Linc had said those words
to her.

The thought of Linc waiting downstairs, however,
offered no solace. A familiar anger grew within her.
Damn him, why had he come? His return was already

stirring up old feelings, old ghosts she didn't want to face.

What would he do if she didn't go down? Would he see himself out? She frowned. No amount of wishful thinking would send Linc on his way tonight. He was clearly determined to settle the matter of those wretched dividend checks.

She pressed a kiss to Joshua's soft cheek, then straightened. Before she could call it a day, there was a dragon in her living room who needed banishing. When she went downstairs, Erin found said dragon staring broodingly at the framed photographs on the fireplace mantel.

She paused on the bottom step. Linc stood in profile, one hand shoved into a pocket, his suit jacket pushed carelessly aside. His wide forehead was creased in concentration, and his moody gaze moved from picture to picture.

He looked so alone, so isolated from the smiling faces staring at him from happier times. Erin noticed he looked longest at the center photograph, the one that had been taken in college when Linc, his brother, Steve, and Merrill had been roommates.

She had been the photographer and remembered the day vividly. It had been a few weeks after she and Merrill had announced their engagement—on a snowy afternoon in another lifetime when three laughing young men had built a giant snowman on the front lawn of her college dorm.

Her throat tightened. They had been so young, so buoyed up by enthusiasm and innocence, never knowing, never suspecting that life would tamper with their secure worlds.

"I remember when you took that picture," Linc said, without taking his eyes from it.

Silently Erin joined him at the fireplace.

"You were bent out of shape at all three of us that day," he continued.

She looked at him in surprise. "No, I wasn't."

"Yes, you were," he corrected, turning to face her. "You and Merrill were supposed to go to some get-together at your parent's place, and Merrill showed up with Steve and me."

His words nudged a long-ago memory. "It was my folks' twenty-fifth wedding anniversary—they were having an open house."

"And Merrill wanted to play in the snow. You were all dressed up and wouldn't join us."

"And I took the picture because—"

"You wanted to show us how stupid we looked—"

"All covered in snow, acting like maniacs."

She looked at the picture again. Three laughing young men—all tall, all handsome, each wearing about ten pounds of snow.

She had been jealous, she remembered now. Merrill's bond with the Severance brothers had seemed an insurmountable obstacle. She had wanted her fiancé all to herself. Looking back on it, her feelings seemed childishly shallow. She had taken the picture through brimming tears because they were going to be late for her mother's and father's anniversary party.

"They were simpler times, weren't they, Linc?"

He turned and faced her. "Were they?"

No answer came. She searched for something to say that might forestall the subject of the dividend checks. She wasn't ready to pick up the threads of another argument.

"Are your parents well?"

"Well enough," she answered softly.

"Steve mentioned your father's retiring from the ministry."

She sighed. "Not exactly. Steve's right that Dad is giving up his calling here, but he's not retiring."

"What's he going to do?"

"Fly three thousand miles to a village in southern Mexico."

"Didn't the Catholics already beat him there by a few centuries?"

At Linc's wry question, she smiled reluctantly. "He wants to build a medical clinic."

"And you're going to miss him and your mother," Linc surmised, his voice surprisingly gentle.

Erin looked past Linc. "I know it's selfish of me, but I will miss them."

Flushing, Erin broke off. The vulnerable tone of her words embarrassed her. A sense of foreboding stirred. This was how it had been between her and Linc. Before he always had been able to get her to open up to him.

"If Dad finds out you're in town, you'll probably be invited to his farewell sermon this Sunday," she continued with forced brightness. "He'll be looking for donations to further the cause."

"I wouldn't be surprised."

Erin flushed again. Her father never hesitated to solicit contributions for his endless charities.

Charity. She had struggled throughout her child-hood to come to terms with that word. For her it had been much easier to give than receive. Accepting the secondhand dresses she'd seen other girls wearing at school had severely trounced her youthful pride. She'd vowed that when she grew up she would *never* accept charity again—in any form. She had promised herself that she would be completely self-sufficient.

Erin's chin angled upward. "Are you going to bring up those dividend checks again?"

"The subject is far from settled, but it's late." He paused. For a long moment his gaze moved over her. "And you look..."

Linc's probing stare made Erin self-conscious about the slim suede skirt and silk and lace blouse she wore. "How do I look?" she asked defensively.

His eyes darkened. "Oh, you look good, but if you're not careful, these late nights will catch up with you."

The last thing Erin wanted from Linc Severance was advice. "News flash, Linc—I can take care of myself."

Something dangerous glinted in his dark gaze. "So you've been telling me, but there's some things a man needs to see for himself."

She opened her mouth to tell him she didn't want or need the services of a watchdog. A wide yawn caught her by surprise. Heat crawled to her cheeks.

She put her hand over her mouth and silently dared him to say something sarcastic. He continued to regard her with his irritating half-smile—a smile that bespoke of male forbearance for female weakness.

Pointedly, he glanced at his watch. "It's getting late—we'll continue this discussion tomorrow."

"Can't," she replied succinctly. "I'm busy."

"Another date?" His voice was low, pulsing with tension.

"You bet—I've got men stacked up to the rafters." It was a childish thing to say, but Linc's proprietary attitude rankled. He needed to be taken down a peg—or ten.

"Then I'd better show up early."

"Suit yourself, but I won't be here."

"Erin, we don't need a board meeting to settle this." The corners of his mouth twisted downward. "Look at it this way—the sooner we hash this out, the sooner I'll be out of your life again."

A throbbing silence pulsed between them. She noticed the fatigue that etched his eyes and the tightness that thinned his lips. Didn't he know how his words hurt her, that the last thing she wanted was him out of her life...forever?

With a start, she realized he couldn't possibly know any such thing, because she hadn't known it until this moment. Wearily, she brushed a hand against her forehead.

"I jog around six each morning. If you insist on having this discussion, come around ten—but I'll warn you right now, my mind is made up."

He nodded briskly and turned to the door. Suddenly it seemed there were no more words to be said between them. Linc had achieved a surrender of sorts and now obviously he had other places to go.

When Erin closed the door behind him, she couldn't resist pushing aside a corner of the drapes. Linc headed toward a car parked across the street. Again, she was struck by how alone he seemed. Alone—complete in and of himself.

The engine turned over, and she flicked off the porch light. Then Erin moved through the living room, turning off lamps as she went. She was feeling very much alone, and the darkened house seemed to call up memories of how it had been before Linc had walked out of her life.

In the wake of Merrill's death, Linc had moved into a spare bedroom. Overwhelmed by shock and an unshakable sense of guilt at her husband's death, she had accepted Linc's presence as a fact of life. In the year he'd been away, however, the naturalness of their relationship had vanished. A pang of regret cut through Erin. The man had been her best friend and now he seemed almost a stranger.

She stepped into her bedroom, not bothering to turn on a lamp. Enough moonlight spilled through the bedroom windows for her to navigate. Besides, the darkness suited her pensive mood.

She slipped off her clothes and pulled on a nightgown. The soft cotton soothed her skin. She moved to the tall windows that overlooked the patio. Absently she parted the sheer draperies. It seemed a time for looking beyond herself. The crescent moon diffused stark light across her backyard and swimming pool. A rippling imitation of the moon floated upon the pool's dark surface. Because she knew there would be more warm days ahead, she'd put off having the pool drained.

She was tempted to go down for a swim. It was a mild night, and the pool was heated. Leaning forward, she pressed her forehead against the windowpane. Her restless energy caught her by surprise.

Usually she fell into bed exhausted at night. Now

she was keyed up and ready for physical activity. It would be hours before she could release that energy by jogging.

Where had her fatigue gone? Lately she had felt exhausted by the simplest acts of daily living. All at once, Erin realized she felt more alive than she had in months.

Linc was back...

# Chapter Two

Early the next morning, Erin hurriedly pulled on a pair of pink shorts. She was running behind schedule. In a few minutes, Kristi would be knocking at the kitchen door.

Not surprisingly, Erin had lain awake much of the night thinking about Linc and the strange role he'd played in her life. When she'd finally managed to drift off, her alarm had awakened her from a dream-disturbed sleep.

Reaching for the white T-shirt on the bed, she spared the room an assessing glance. Everything looked reasonably tidy. She poked her head through the shirt and gave the room a second look.

Even here, Erin was made reluctantly aware of Linc's influence. During her marriage to Merrill, this was not the bedroom they had shared. This room was smaller, cozier and devoid of intimate memories. Linc had moved her things into it during the days immediately following her husband's death.

As she bent to tie her shoelaces, Erin considered Linc's actions from the time he'd joined her at the hospital until the night he'd walked out of her life. She was forced to admit that he'd probably saved her sanity. She'd been close to the edge. Linc's compassion, his knowing the right words to say, had pulled her from that frightening precipice.

She straightened, again uncomfortably aware of how heavily she'd leaned upon Linc. She'd allowed him to become the caretaker of her grief. His strength had permitted her to be weak. Their relationship during those weeks had been more intensely intimate than any she'd shared with another person. He'd held her endlessly, whispered words of hope...

With a sigh, Erin brought herself to the present and stepped into the bathroom. As she reached for the hairbrush, the sight of her pale reflection staring at her awakened a fragment of memory—one she hadn't thought about in more than a year. Linc had brushed her hair. He'd also seen to other, more personal needs.

How had she managed to forget the times he'd cooked for her, helped her dress, even helped her bathe? Heat rushed through her. How could memories so visceral have lain dormant all this time? Running the brush through her shoulder-length hair, Erin realized that the weeks after Merrill's death had been a black void she'd been afraid to probe. She'd suppressed all thoughts about that desperate time in her life, but now those thoughts were rushing back to her.

She reached for an elastic band to hold her hair. No wonder Linc had left town. He'd needed to find breathing space in order to live his own life. She flicked off the light and headed downstairs, barely reaching the kitchen before hearing Kristi's knock.

Erin opened the back door and smiled at the teenager dressed in faded jeans and an oversize orange T-shirt with the words Porpoise Power stenciled across its front.

"Hi, Mrs. Clay."

"Good morning, Kristi. I appreciate you being so prompt on a Saturday morning."

The girl stepped into the kitchen. "No problem."

Before Erin could close the door, Linc Severance materialized on the back step. Erin blinked twice, just to make sure he wasn't a lingering afterimage from the dreams he'd sauntered through last night.

He didn't disappear, and she glared at him. This was becoming a habit—first her front door, now the back one. "What are you doing here?"

"Joining you, obviously."

That was direct enough. Her eyes narrowed. "Why?"

"Simple matter of unfinished business," he answered coolly.

Conscious that Kristi was listening avidly to the exchange, Erin decided to take up her annoyance with Linc outside.

She turned from the six foot plus mountain of aggravation and forced herself to smile at the obviously fascinated teenager. "You know the routine with Joshua."

"Right—if he wakes up before you get back, I'll help him get dressed and fix breakfast."

"Remember to find the less violent cartoons for him to watch."

Kristi flicked her mane of long, golden hair and grinned. "No guns or lasers, right?"

Aware of Linc's thoughtful stare, Erin nodded. Joining him on the step was absolutely the last thing she wanted to do. But since she had no intention of letting Kristi overhear their conversation, there seemed no alternative to doing just that.

The door closed behind them, and Linc moved toward the driveway. His white running shorts and navy blue polo shirt emphasized his lean frame and powerful legs.

A surge of energy flowed through Erin, and she felt the sudden need to move. Instead of the fast-paced activity her body craved, however, she settled for the steady, familiar rhythm of her warm-up stretches. Linc followed suit, and she found her gaze drifting over him. He really was in superb shape. His arms were sculpted with well-defined biceps, his stomach appeared flat, and his legs looked as if they could carry him across a desert without giving out.

"Which way?" Linc asked, finishing his contortions.

Erin's eyes jerked to his. Good grief, she'd been looking at him almost as if he were a...sex object. Her skin flushed with heat. She'd die before letting Linc Severance know that for a few seconds he'd gotten to her physically.

She pointed eastward and began to jog in place. "I usually make a loop around the park. It's not quite six miles."

"Sounds good."

With that, they were off. The sidewalk was wide enough for them to run abreast. The large, well-groomed yards they passed were mostly deserted. Occasionally sprinkler systems had flicked on, and the unsyncopated rhythms of swishing water accompanied the thud of their feet.

Erin sucked in the cool morning air and felt a soothing kind of satisfaction. She'd been jogging for several months now and had become addicted to the mild euphoria that pumped through her when she ran. The sun was just beginning to come up. It was a magical time of day, seemingly filled with an abundance of life's possibilities.

She tried not to let Linc's presence disrupt her fragile mood of well-being. Yet the knowledge that she had merely postponed their confrontation was impossible to forget.

Block after block of sidewalk passed beneath their pounding feet, and soon they were circling Wasatch Park, heading south. She sensed Linc was holding back in order to match her stride.

"If you want to pick up the pace, go ahead, Linc."

"This feels pretty good. I'll stay with you."

*I'll stay with you...*

Without warning, Erin's thoughts tumbled to the night Merrill had died after their last bitter quarrel.

*I'll stay with you...* That was what Linc had told her when he'd shown up at the emergency room. Why had it seemed so natural to turn to him? There had been other people in her life from whom she could have sought support. Why had she depended upon Linc to navigate through the turbulent waters of her grief?

Determinedly Erin pushed aside the dark thoughts, finding it was easier to do so now than in the past. It was a beautiful September morning. She was alive and had a precious little boy waiting at home for her.

Why torture herself about a man who no longer wanted to be a part of her life? She gave in to the sudden need to pick up the pace. Linc easily matched the new rhythm. Glancing at him, she noticed that his chest rose and fell evenly, giving no indication he was exerting himself. As far as she could tell, he hadn't even worked up a sweat.

He turned his head, his dark eyes locking briefly with hers. A tiny frisson of awareness rippled through her. She jerked her gaze from him and with a burst of adrenaline pounded the pavement for all she was worth. She didn't look back. The feeling that she was on the verge of a disturbing discovery nipped at her heels, a discovery she wasn't ready to face, and for as long as she could, she intended to postpone it.

The sun had risen fully by the time they reached her house. She paused on the step. Her T-shirt was damp from her exertions and clung to her with un-nerving transparency. She didn't look at Linc as they walked into the kitchen.

Kristi greeting them at the door. "How was the run?"

"Fine," Erin said briskly, trying to block out Linc's disturbing proximity. "Is Joshua up?"

Kristi stretched before answering. "I checked on him twice. He's still zonked out."

Erin reached for her purse on the counter and quickly counted out the teenager's payment. "I really appreciate you sitting for me so early."

The girl slipped the money into a pocket of her

jeans. "I appreciate the work—I'm saving for a new tape deck. See you tomorrow."

The door closed behind Kristi with a solid click. Trying to ignore Linc's unsettling nearness, Erin looked at the clock on the microwave. "I'm going to shower before I wake up Joshua."

"A shower sounds good—mind if I use the downstairs bathroom?"

The sudden image of Linc standing in the shower with soapy water cascading down him snaked through her mind. "Go ahead—I've got a few minutes before I start breakfast."

"Am I invited?"

She frowned at him in exasperation. He was the most stubborn man she'd ever met. Knowing him, he would stay and wear her down until they'd settled the matter of the dividend checks.

"It's Saturday, Linc. I want to enjoy the day with my son, not spend it arguing about Merrill's share of Prestige Builders."

"We could declare a truce until Monday," he suggested reasonably.

"Ah, but would you stick to it?"

"Depends on my incentive—what's for breakfast?"

It would have been easy to let him charm her into believing his intentions were friendly, but Erin knew Linc well enough to know he had business on his mind. "We're having something low in fat and high in nutritional value."

"I can hardly wait."

*I can,* Erin thought, wanting and needing a respite

from Linc's continued company. She made it to the bottom of the stairs before his voice stopped her.

"Erin..."

She looked over her shoulder. "Yes?"

"I won't railroad you into doing anything you don't want to."

She smiled determinedly. "You're right about that."

Later, after showering and dressing, Erin opened the red blinds in Joshua's bedroom. Morning sunlight filtered into the room she had redecorated several weeks earlier.

The new slate blue carpeting contrasted cleanly against the white walls. She'd painted his bed, dresser and bookcase white, also. Red accents were provided by an enormous fire truck, a basketball hoop and a picture of a hot air balloon. She was pleased that only *new* things filled the room.

The increased light in Joshua's room produced no discernible movement beneath his denim bedspread. Erin smiled philosophically, reminding herself that one of the things she'd always appreciated about her son was that he was a late sleeper. Still, routines were important.

She leaned down and gently shook his shoulder. "Joshua..."

His eyes opened sleepily. He blinked twice and then was fully awake. "Is it time for preschool?"

"That's Monday, honey. Today's Saturday."

"Is it Smurfs yet?"

"Almost, but you have to get dressed and have breakfast first."

Joshua pushed back his covers and scrambled from the bed. His small bare feet virtually danced against the carpet. "Where's my stuff?"

Erin smiled and pointed to a small stack of folded clothes on the red cushion of his captain's chair. "Fresh underwear, jeans, shirt and socks."

Joshua raced to the chair and rooted out his underwear. The neat stack of garments deteriorated into assorted lumps.

"Slow down, honey—it's still early. Besides, you need to visit the bathroom, don't you?"

Her question produced an immediate reaction. Her son paused, his eyes widening. Then he was off like a shot to the hall bathroom.

"I'll be downstairs, making breakfast," Erin called after him.

Linc sat at the table and sipped the fresh-squeezed orange juice Erin had set before him while studying his surroundings. Rumpled pages of childish scrawls decorated her refrigerator. Canning jars filled with tomatoes covered the countertop over the dishwasher. Seed catalogs, sewing patterns and a skein of blue yarn poked from a white wicker basket on another counter. As always, Erin seemed in the midst of several projects.

He had no intention of letting himself be charmed by the mildly chaotic ambience of her cluttered kitchen. He'd come here today for another reason. Linc's gaze came to rest upon Joshua. The boy was waiting impatiently for his breakfast so he could watch the Smurfs on TV. Linc reminded himself that the money Erin was so foolishly refusing to accept would benefit Merrill's son.

As she shuttled between fridge, stove and table, Linc felt the weight of Joshua's guarded stare. Linc curbed his disappointment that the boy didn't remember him or the times they'd spent together before Linc had left for Los Angeles. It unnerved him that Joshua looked at him without a flicker of recognition.

Erin carried a steaming pot from the stove to the table. "Relax, Josh, you've got fifteen minutes before the Smurfs start."

Linc studied the clean line of her profile. After her shower, she hadn't bothered with makeup. He noticed a faint smattering of freckles dusting the delicate bridge of her nose. The scent of soap and something essentially feminine drifted to him.

"Are Jeremy and Jordan coming to preschool tomorrow, too, Mommy?"

"Not tomorrow," Erin corrected softly. "It's the day *after* tomorrow—and yes, Jeremy and Jordan will be there."

Linc watched Erin spoon an unfamiliar gray mixture into his and Joshua's bowls. "Jeremy and Jordan?" he asked, seeking entry to the conversation.

"Joshua's two best friends," Erin explained, her brown eyes warming. "You've heard of the me generation? I think we've entered the J generation. Joshua also has friends named Jason, Jenny, Jill, Jared, Johnny, Joseph, Justin and Jesse."

Joshua reached for a small cup of raisins and began sprinkling them onto the glop in his bowl. "You forgot Jake—*he's* my bestest friend."

"And Jake," Erin added, taking her place at the table.

Reluctantly, Linc found himself intrigued—both by the conversation and the mortarlike mass Erin had served him. "So what's preschool?"

"It comes before kindergarten," she explained.

Linc nodded as if she stated the obvious and reached for his spoon. He took a conservative taste of what he'd concluded must be oatmeal.

All the saliva in his mouth seemed to disappear. He had no idea how he was going to choke down one mouthful of the god-awful stuff, let alone finish an entire bowl.

Calling upon the self-control he used to carry him through high-stake business negotiations, Linc kept his features neutral, swallowed and reached for his glass of juice.

He realized he had both Erin's and Joshua's undivided attention.

"Linc, wouldn't you like some sugar or milk with that?" Erin asked.

Looking at their bowls, he realized there was more to eating the unpalatable mixture then he'd realized. As he drowned the stuff with milk, his gaze was pulled to Erin. Quiet amusement and another emotion he couldn't identify stared at him. He swore silently. He was so damned tired of being drawn against his will by the subtle mystique of Erin Clay's femininity.

He forced himself to concentrate on taking another spoonful of what she'd served him. The taste of sweet, warming milk and brown sugar soothed his offended taste buds. He looked up. "It's oatmeal, right?"

"Yeah," Joshua said, watching him as if Linc were a vacationing alien—and a not very bright one at that.

Linc discovered it was a humbling experience to be put in one's place by a four-year-old.

As breakfast continued, a twinge of sadness pricked Linc. Merrill would never again experience the simple pleasure of sharing a meal with his family. Linc shifted, uncomfortable with the thought that he was an interloper, stealing something that rightfully belonged to another.

When Joshua was finished eating, he hopped off his chair and headed toward the family room. "Is it on the right channel, Mommy?"

Erin joined her son. "Let's check."

Watching Joshua, Linc realized that while he'd been away, the boy had grown from a somewhat chubby toddler into a wiry four-year-old. Linc's gaze went to Erin as she trailed after her son. Her silky brown hair swayed gently against the back of the light blue shirt she'd put on after her shower.

He stared after her, appreciating the snug fit of her jeans. When he realized what he was doing, Linc swore succinctly. Some things never changed. Like the way Erin Clay's long legs looked in denim—or shorts. Or the way he reacted whenever he was around her.

Linc pushed that thought away and stood. From the family room, he heard the sound of Erin's laughter in response to something her son was telling her.

The first time he'd met Erin she'd been laughing at one of Merrill's jokes. For no reason he could understand, Linc had bristled with impatience.

He hadn't liked her initially, he remembered. When

challenged by Steve and Merrill to explain his reservations, Linc had felt uncomfortably defensive. He'd been unable to put into words what it was about Erin that rubbed him the wrong way.

He'd told himself her spontaneity was immature, her bubbling optimism foolish. He'd told himself she was too unsophisticated and unpolished for Merrill. Hell, he'd told himself her lustrous, dark hair was probably dyed, her wide, brown eyes the result of contacts and her glowing skin... Because she'd worn no makeup, he had been hard put to figure out how she'd managed the flawless complexion.

Linc began to pace. It had been when Erin was pregnant that he had finally admitted to himself her softness appealed to him. That had been a milestone in their relationship—the beginning of him coming to terms with his ambivalent feelings toward Merrill's wife.

Linc paused, absently fingering the soft blue yarn on the counter. He'd never *loved* her. An honorable man wouldn't allow himself to love his best friend's wife. He had...cared for Erin. Something about her stirred something within him. But it wasn't love.

How could it have been? From the first time Merrill had introduced them, she had belonged to his friend and had therefore been irrevocably forbidden to Linc.

Later, when Merrill, Steve and he had gone into business together, it had been impossible for Linc to cut her from his life. During that period, he'd dated a lot of different women. Looking... He had been looking for someone who could make him feel what Erin did. He was still looking. The thought startled him.

When he realized he was stroking the blue yarn as he yearned to stroke Erin, Linc jerked his hand away, resorting again to pacing. Over time, he'd managed to reconcile his feelings for his late friend's wife. He'd convinced himself that his concern was brotherly. When Erin had been pregnant with Joshua, Linc had made a point of being there for her. He'd told himself that she was the sister he'd never had.

When Merrill, Steve and he had debated who should manage their new Los Angeles branch of the business, Linc had jumped at the chance. He'd wanted to put some distance between himself and Erin. Then one black night Merrill had driven his car into a tree. Linc happened to be in town at the time and had charged to Erin's side and in the process become involved in a cover-up to protect Erin from the seamy details of her husband's death. Immediately Linc had found himself sucked into the familiar whirlpool of his complex feelings for Erin.

Under the circumstances, his concern had been natural, acceptable. Unlikely as it seemed, she'd become as close a friend to him as Merrill had once been. Linc was able to accept Erin's friendship—as long as he remained convinced he wasn't attracted to her physically. And convinced he'd been—until the night she'd fallen asleep in his arms. Linc had dozed off, too. When he had awakened, he'd been caressing her breast.

That was when Linc had understood that his feelings for Erin did not end at simple friendship. And in all the years he'd known her, he'd been lying to himself. Not about loving her, but about desiring her. In his own way, Linc was as much a fraud as Merrill had been. He shoved his hands into his pockets. One thing was certain, he sure as hell wasn't any white knight.

"Don't worry, Papa Smurf will save them."

Erin's voice jerked Linc to the present—with a vengeance. As she came into the kitchen, he noticed her smile faltered, then faded. Coldness unraveled in his chest. It was clear she would never forgive him for running out on her last year. He told himself that was good—her negative feelings gave him the self-control he needed to keep his hands off her.

Erin might not realize it, but her anger was doing them both a favor. And, if he was smart, Linc would keep stoking the flames of that anger.

*Chapter Three*

With Josh mesmerized by an enchanted forest populated with little blue people, Erin returned to the kitchen. The first thing to catch her attention was a glowering Linc Severance.

She stiffened automatically. Who'd asked him to stay for breakfast and suffer through a meal he'd obviously loathed? It didn't improve her mood to recall that *she* had invited him. Even so, no one had held a gun to his head and forced him to stay.

Scowling, she moved to the table. "Are you still here?"

At the tactless question, she saw his frown fade. The man elevated contrary to new heights.

"We can talk while I help with the dishes."

*Talk or badger me about those damned dividend checks while flaunting yourself?* Erin's thoughts brought her up short. After his shower, Linc had changed into gray slacks and a white shirt. Though it might annoy her that he'd been so sure of his welcome he had brought a change of clothes, he was hardly flaunting himself.

Impatient with herself for remembering too accurately how good he'd looked jogging, Erin began gathering up the cereal bowls. "I don't want your help."

"Two will get the job done twice as fast," he pointed out blandly.

What was with him? The angrier—the *meaner*—she became, the more satisfied he seemed.

"Look, I don't know what's going on here, but this is my kitchen and..."

He began collecting silverware from the table. "It always was tough winning an argument with you."

She started in surprise. "You and I never argued."

"Think back to the time you were pregnant with Joshua and you ran yourself ragged trying to hold down a job, keep house, make baby clothes and decorate a nursery fit for the offspring of royalty." His observation simmered with disapproval.

"Merrill was away a lot. I had to pick up the slack," she countered, trying to keep the defensiveness from her voice.

Linc's expression clouded. "Lucky for you I was around to keep you in line."

Had Linc Severance always been so obnoxious and she'd just never noticed it before? "The women in my family have a tradition of turning into blimps after the fourth month. I had to get everything done while I was still capable of movement."

Linc's troubled gaze dropped from her face to take

in the rest of her. "When you were six months along, you hardly showed."

Beneath her clothes—beneath her skin—Erin felt a tingling warmth. She could feel the mood between them altering subtly, drifting inexorably toward a level of intimacy that had once seemed so natural between them. She fought valiantly against the treacherous memories.

"But by month seven, I looked as if I'd swallowed a beach ball."

For a moment his compelling stare warmed, holding her transfixed. "A very small, very firm beach ball."

"Uh, thanks."

"As compliments go, that wasn't one of my best."

"The thanks is for being there the night I had Joshua."

The warmth vanished from Linc's gaze. "I think that's the only time in my life I've been really afraid."

"You...yelled at me," Erin recalled, moving to the sink. "I was in labor, and you yelled at me."

"I couldn't believe you were stupid enough to wait for Merrill to get home before doing something."

"It was a month before my due date—I didn't think I was really having the baby. Besides, Merrill had said he would be home early."

"When I showed up, you were alone and in hard labor." A mild ferocity sharpened Linc's features. "You scared the hell out of me, lady."

"By the time you arrived, I was pretty scared myself."

The long-ago hurt of her husband missing their

son's birth because he had run out of gas on a back country road still touched a raw nerve with Erin. It had been Linc who'd stayed with her in the labor room until her mother and father had arrived.

It had been Linc who had paced the hospital corridors until Joshua was born. It had been Linc, not Merrill, who had first seen their new son.

"So who was he?"

"He—who?" Erin asked blankly.

"The Casanova coming on to you last night at your front door."

It astonished Erin that in three seconds she could go from feeling tender and nostalgic to furious. She turned the faucet on full force and reached for the liquid detergent. "His name is Paul, and you're overstating what happened."

Linc slid the bowl into the foaming water. "He had his hands all over you."

"I would have handled the situation without your interference."

Until now, Erin had forgotten that Linc had no business ordering one of her dates to leave.

"It's you thinking you can take care of yourself that worries me."

"Just what are you afraid of?" Erin ruthlessly scrubbed a bowl. "That I'm such a pea brain I'm going to let some pervert on the make have his evil way with me?"

Linc's fingers closed around her arm, and he turned her to face him. His features were as grim as those of a judge passing sentence. "This is no joking matter."

"I can take care of myself," she snapped impatiently. "I'm a mother, for Pete's sake."

Linc's dark eyes glittered. "That's supposed to make you invincible? Being a mother?"

She pulled her arm free. "You should know I'm not the emotional dishrag I was a year ago, Linc. I'm a lot tougher now."

His eyes flicked up and down her. "I've seen newborn chicks tougher than you, honey."

"So what do you want me to do, Linc? Challenge you to an arm-wrestling match to prove I'm some sort of macho woman?"

His lips twitched suspiciously, infuriating Erin. Suddenly it became essential that she demonstrate she was no longer weak, that she could indeed take care of herself. A newborn chick, ha!

She returned her attention to the soaking bowls and attacked them with a scrubbing pad while visualizing herself taking karate lessons, changing flat tires and chopping mounds of firewood.

From the corner of her eye, she watched Linc unbutton his cuffs and roll them back. There was no way she could keep from noticing the dark hairs dusting his forearms. Great, he saw her in chicken feathers while she was becoming increasingly aware of him as a potent male force.

His broad hands slipped into the clear rinse water, and he began retrieving glasses and bowls, stacking them precisely on the plastic dish rack.

"What's wrong with your dishwasher?" he asked.

Erin jumped. She'd become hypnotized by watching his long fingers moving under the rinse water. The tiny black hairs on the back of his knuckles seemed to gleam.

"Uh, I don't know. It stops on the wash cycle and won't drain."

"Have you had someone look at it?"

"Mr. Lucco's on his second honeymoon. I'll call him when he gets back."

"Mr. Lucco?"

"He owns a little repair store in the old shopping center."

"Why not call someone else?"

Erin tore her gaze from Linc's hands. "Mr. Lucco is a darling little man who does excellent work. I wouldn't dream of calling anyone else."

"I don't think he expects you to wait for him to get back from his vacation before you get your dishwasher fixed," Linc said impatiently.

"Maybe not, but I have the feeling he needs all the business he can get."

Linc muttered something that Erin couldn't quite catch. It didn't matter. The dishwasher could wait for Mr. Lucco to get back from Greece.

It amazed Erin how keenly she resented Linc's predisposition to interfere in her life. As far as she was concerned, she'd done a damn fair job of putting the pieces of that life together after he had chosen to disappear from it.

When the dishes were washed, dried and put away, Erin waited for Linc to say goodbye and take his act on the road. Naturally he did nothing of the kind.

"So what's next on your schedule?" he inquired as if their being together was a normal occurrence.

"Joshua and I are going to work in the garden."

"This very minute?"

His question made her wary. "When the cartoon show he's watching is over."

"How long will that take?"

She glanced at the clock. "About fifteen minutes."

"That's all the time I need."

"If you're bringing up what I think you're bringing up, I want you to leave."

His eyebrows rode low over his eyes. "Erin, you know why I'm here, and you're making this tougher than it has to be. I have some papers in the car—"

"Get out."

"You're being unreasonable."

"Get out. I told you I didn't want to talk about—"

Whatever patience Linc might have been exercising disappeared abruptly. "Listen, you little spitfire, I've got better things to do than cater to your sensibilities. Joshua needs—"

She jabbed her forefinger at Linc's wide chest. "*I* decide what Joshua needs. And it isn't charity, not from you—not from anyone."

"It's not charity," Linc returned with a low growl of annoyance. "You and Joshua are entitled to Merrill's share."

"That's ridiculous. You and Steve are doing all the work now."

"Aside from the legalities that factor into this, Merrill would have wanted you to—"

"It's not right," Erin interrupted starkly.

Linc's dark eyes smoldered. "Why, dammit?"

"Because...because we don't need any money. Merrill had a huge life insurance policy, the house is paid for and I don't have a lot of expenses. Joshua and I are doing fine—better than fine.''

"Merrill invested thousands of dollars in Prestige Builders," Linc reminded her. "By the terms of the incorporation agreement, that money—plus a percentage of the business—is legally yours.''

Erin raised her chin. In her mind she saw every ill-fitting hand-me-down dress she'd ever worn. All of them represented a vulnerability she never wanted to experience again, especially in regards to Linc. "If you keep sending those checks, I'll burn them.''

He ran a hand through his hair. "God, you're stubborn.''

"It doesn't matter what your lawyer or anyone else thinks," Erin said. "I've taken charge of my life. No one is going to tell me what I can and cannot do.''

"That sounds like a challenge," he pointed out, his voice low.

"Take it any way you want—I stand on my own two feet.''

"I'll tell you how I'd like to take it." Something other than anger pulsated in his stormy gaze. His hands seemed to come from nowhere and descend on her shoulders. "Right here. Right now.''

Suddenly Erin was in Linc's arms with his mouth a scant inch from hers. She knew her eyes must be huge. She couldn't catch her breath.

Linc seemed to be everywhere. His stark nearness made her heart pound. The dark shadow of a morning beard hovered an inch from her face. The rasp of stubble looked unapologetically male, rough and... and strangely beckoning.

His hard angles crowded against her. Beneath the

angles, she sensed the muscle and sinew of a man in his prime. His freshly showered scent carried a faint muskiness that sent a shimmering arc of awareness through her.

Breathless, she met his hard stare. Had she ever been this close to him before? For the first time she noticed that his dark eyes had tiny flecks of black scattered through them. Her glance lowered to his mouth. She licked her suddenly dry lips.

The silence spun out between them. They had all the time in the world to close the puny distance separating them.

*Do it...* From some reckless region of her mind, the words took shape, an invitation to partake of the madness Linc's mouth so temptingly offered.

"Do you have any idea how you tempt me, Erin?"

Numbly, she shook her head. Or at least she thought she did. Maybe she remained frozen in his arms, waiting for history to rewrite itself between them. Erin and Linc gazed at each other. Then, slowly, painfully, Linc relaxed his hold and stepped back.

The telephone—ringing on the wall next to them—and Joshua—calling simultaneously from the family room—catapulted time into motion. Dazed, they remained where they were for several seconds.

Automatically Erin's hand reached for the phone. "Hello."

Linc's hot gaze pinned her in place. "I'll check on Joshua," he said evenly.

She stared after him, barely aware of the voice in her ear.

"Dear, are you there?"

Finally her mother's words registered. "Yes—yes, I'm here."

"I'm just calling to let you know I'll be later than I thought today. Don't expect me before noon."

"That's all right," Erin said, trying to collect her scattered thoughts. "We haven't been out to the garden yet—Josh is still watching cartoons."

"Mrs. Mahoney really appreciates the extra produce you've given her this summer. This is the first year she hasn't had a garden, you know."

Erin thought of the eighty-year-old woman who'd broken her hip this spring. "I bet she plants one next year."

Her mother chuckled. "I bet she does, at that. See you later, honey."

"Bye." Slowly, Erin hung up the phone. Her thoughts were not on the brief conversation she'd shared with her mother but instead revolved around what had almost happened between herself and Linc.

*A kiss?* Obviously. Yet from Linc's furious expression as he'd stalked off, it was a kiss he'd regretted before it had even begun. She winced. What right did he have to be angry? He was the one who'd barged into her life. He was the one who'd pulled her into his arms. He was the one who'd... She swallowed. He was the one who'd drawn away first.

Linc watched a battalion of little blue rodents scatter before a giant orange cat. He identified with the cat—who was big and strong yet couldn't master creatures half his size.

And the cat was hungry.

He glanced at Joshua. The boy had wanted his

mother to see a commercial about some new kind of cereal. Linc wished the kid luck. Erin didn't look like the kind of mother who could be talked into putting anything called Bubble Gum Buddies into her grocery cart.

*You almost kissed her.*

Shell-shocked, Linc sat on the couch and stared unseeingly at the television. He had come within a heartbeat of acting upon a desire that had been building for years. His hands clenched.

Dammit, he'd come to get her out of his life or, more accurately, out of his mind. Hadn't he? His thoughts ground onward. Erin hadn't looked as if she was going to stop him. Instead, she'd looked soft, and dewy and...ready. He closed his eyes and called up the sizzling image of her face tilted toward his, her lips parted invitingly, her eyelids drifting downward...

"Are you asleep, mister?"

Linc's eyes jerked opened. Joshua's small face peered curiously at him. "No."

"You look asleep."

"I was resting my eyes."

"Are you done?"

Linc nodded, noticing the TV had been turned off. "Did the cat ever catch those little blue demons?"

"'Course not," the boy answered, edging back.

"Too bad," Linc grumbled, getting to his feet.

Joshua tilted his head at him. "He's not supposed to catch 'em, mister."

"The name's Linc."

"That's a funny name."

"Thanks, kid."

Erin entered the room. "Are you ready to tackle the garden, sport?"

"Can I hoe?"

"Not today, honey. We're pulling the rest of the corn."

The boy jumped up and down. "Goody."

Linc's gaze followed the kid's animated movements. He hadn't realized how much energy a four-year-old had at his command. "Is someone coming to help you?"

Erin turned on him, her eyes flashing. "Linc, I'm not plowing the west forty."

He shoved his hands into his pockets so he wouldn't do something rash—like shake her, or pull her into his arms and—

"I'm helping," Joshua pointed out, a miniature replica of his mother's stubbornness.

"If you need an extra pair of hands, I'm available." He didn't know what prompted him to make the offer. Perhaps it was simply a case of atoning for his reckless action in the kitchen.

Erin shrugged. "Come along if you want to."

Two hours later, Linc had a host of new questions to mull over. He decided that Erin couldn't have worked any harder if she did have forty acres under cultivation. Her garden was precisely laid out, huge, and he hadn't seen a weed with the temerity to encroach upon the neatly tilled rows holding her produce.

The woman was a gardening general. And damned if Joshua wasn't just like her, hauling out long ears of perfectly shaped corn by the armful and depositing them into a large aluminum tub.

They worked well together—mother and son—marching here and there, pointing out the progress of a pumpkin named Horatio and a sunflower tall enough to interfere with air traffic. Linc pitched in as best he could, moving through the neat rows, astonished that Erin and Joshua had maintained such a big garden.

Somewhere along the line, he realized that most of his tension had ebbed, that he liked being outdoors. The garden was a quiet place, a place where he could let his thoughts roam undisturbed. Being in the dirt and touching the raw produce made him speculate about his ancestors. They'd been farmers, or were they ranchers? Stretching, Linc wiped his brow and wondered what the first symptoms were for a mid-life crisis.

And always, Erin loomed on the periphery of his vision—unsettling the peace that almost hovered within touching distance. Slim-hipped, long-legged and softly ripe, she tugged at something primitive in him. If Joshua weren't here, Linc would have liked to lay her down on the soft grass and strip away her clothing and...

He brought himself up with a snarl. Gardens were dangerous places. They were highly erotic and...and gave a man too much opportunity to think. About his woman.

Linc dropped more corn into the tub. *Wrong*—not his woman. Never his woman. He reminded himself again that there was no place in his life for Merrill's widow.

When Erin's mother, Claire, pulled into the driveway in her vintage car, Linc felt as if he'd been granted a reprieve from his aching awareness of Erin.

Smiling, the older woman stepped from the car. Like a miniature tornado, Joshua hurled toward her. "Grandma, guess what I done?"

Heedless of her beige dress slacks, the slender woman knelt beside the boy and hugged him. "What did you do, honey?"

"I pulled all the corn!"

Claire laughed in delight. "I'm proud of you."

The older woman's hair was dark and vibrant, and her face glowed with good health. Linc didn't think he'd ever seen anyone who looked less like his mental idea of a grandmother.

Erin came toward them, lugging the metal tub overflowing with corn. Linc strode toward her. "Put that down—it's too heavy."

At Linc's growl, Erin glared. When was he going to learn he couldn't order her around? "It's not too heavy. I—"

He lifted the container from her. "Shut up, Erin."

She blinked twice, not sure she'd heard him correctly.

"Who do you think you are?" she called after him as he carried the tub to the trunk of her mother's car. His pace didn't slacken, even though she was sure he heard her.

"Hello, dear."

Erin glanced at her mother. "That man is pushy beyond belief."

Her mother smiled serenely. "He's just being helpful, honey."

"*Helpful?*" Erin frowned. "What he's being is bossy and overbearing."

Brown eyes very much like her own sparkled mischievously. "He's being a man, dear." Her mother looked at Joshua. "Here, Joshua, give Linc the keys to the trunk."

Josh accepted the jangling keys and raced to the car. "I can't believe how fast he's growing."

With Joshua trailing behind him, Linc joined them. "Here's your keys, Mrs. Conroy—corn's all loaded."

"Thank you, Linc." Her mother looked lovingly at Josh. "And thank *you*, Joshua. Would you like to come with Grandma to drop off the corn? I'll treat you to a hamburger."

Josh's eyes danced as he looked expectantly at Erin. "Can I, Mommy? Can I?"

"Of course you can, honey."

Claire held out her hand to Josh. "Where do you want to go for your hamburger?"

Without hesitation, Josh named the golden arches. In a matter of minutes, Erin found herself alone with an unsmiling Linc Severance. So what else was new?

She set a hose running in the garden, looked longingly at the pool and headed for the house. There was no way she was going to indulge in a swim with Linc around. The thought of him seeing her in a skimpy swimsuit put her on edge. The thought of seeing him in a swimsuit...

There were just some things a woman shouldn't think about.

She stepped into the dining room where she'd left last night's paper. When Linc joined Erin, her nerves seemed to jump to red alert. She desperately needed time away from him to make sense of what had almost happened between them in the kitchen.

"I always liked this room," he said gruffly.

Uneasily, her glance shied from him, and she sur-
veyed her surroundings. Sunlight flowed through the
sheer dining room draperies, across the cream-colored
carpet to halo the polished pecan table.

Needlepoint cushions that she'd spent hours crewel-
ling and slip-knotting covered the high-backed
chairs. Floral watercolors repeated the same accents
of apricot and gray she'd used in her needlepoint and
the silk flower centerpiece.

"You've got a talent for decorating," he continued,
pulling out the chair next to her. His polite observation carried no hint of the passion that had almost
swallowed them whole.

Feeling cornered, Erin plucked a wooden embroi-
dery hoop from his path and placed the unfinished
project on the table.

She forced herself to relax and tried to tame her
sudden awareness of him. "It—it wasn't easy fur-
nishing the house the way I wanted it. Merrill hired
a decorator with a precise idea of how *she* thought
things should look."

"I remember you having some heated discussion
on the subject with Whitney."

Erin looked at him in surprise. "That was her
name—I'd forgotten. Did she work for you, too?"

He shook his head. "We dated a bit."

Linc Severance and Whitney Stark... Erin sighed
softly. The woman was classically beautiful and
oozed self-confidence.

"I should have guessed you would ask her out."

Curiosity edged Linc's features. "Why is that?"

Erin shifted under his quiet scrutiny. Was he currently between women, or was there someone special

in his life? "No particular reason, other than she was gorgeous."

Linc's features sharpened perceptively. "I guess like most men I'm susceptible to a gorgeous woman."

There was something different about Linc's gaze as he looked at her. She couldn't help thinking about their almost kiss. Now, sitting next to him at her dining room table, she had the strangest feeling that it didn't really matter that they hadn't kissed. Something had altered irrevocably between them.

A part of her mourned the friend she sensed she'd lost. But another part of her was curious about the stranger who'd taken his place.

"Nothing happened, Erin."

Her gaze jerked to his shuttered one. "Wh-what do you mean?"

"You know what I'm talking about," he replied, his tone grim.

She knew her face was red. "Uh, I suppose I do."

"Well, it's nothing to fret over," he continued coolly. "Just a simple case of an attraction almost getting out of hand." He stood. "Have you reconsidered accepting the quarterly dividend payments?"

She had difficulty shifting gears from one subject to the next. "No. My mind is made up."

Her announcement brought a quick frown to his face. "My brother and I didn't get where we are by taking no for an answer."

"Sometimes, Linc, there's no choice."

"Don't bet on it."

# *Chapter Four*

On Sunday afternoon, Linc sat behind the desk that was at once familiar and unfamiliar. As he glanced around his old office, it was difficult to believe an entire year had passed since he'd last been there.

Caught by a spurt of restless energy, he pushed back his chair and stood. He felt as if he'd come full circle. Erin's image crept into his thoughts. Yesterday he'd stood in her kitchen and vowed to use her anger as a shield between them. Scarcely ten minutes had elapsed before he'd found himself pulling her into his arms. His continuing susceptibility to her made a mockery of his determination to overcome his attraction to her.

Dammit, Erin had him behaving like a lovesick teenager. Linc ran a hand through his hair. He hadn't acted like a lovesick teenager even when he'd been in his teens. Now that he had reached his thirties, it was inconceivable that he should be struck by a case of raging hormones. And, despite his reflections in Erin's garden, he was too young for a mid-life crisis.

The door to Linc's office opened, and Steve poked his head in. "So, how's it feel to be back, little brother?"

Despite his gloomy mood, Linc smiled as Steve sauntered into the room. "I thought we settled which one of us was the little brother in my senior year of high school."

A rueful grin tugged at his older brother's mouth. "I was speaking chronologically." Steve claimed the chair across from Linc's desk. "I assume from your scowl when I came in that your meeting with Erin didn't go the way you'd planned."

"Lord, was there ever a more hardheaded woman?"

Steve stretched his long legs in front of him and leaned back in his chair. "You're supposed to be the persuasive brother—why don't you talk to her again?"

Linc glanced at his casually dressed brother. If Linc were the more persuasive of the two, then Steve was definitely the laid back one. Wearing faded jeans and a maroon polo shirt, Steve looked nothing like the president of one of the hottest up-and-coming building companies in the western states.

Linc returned to his desk and sat in the chair across from his brother. "Erin's not in the mood to listen to reason. She has some harebrained idea that accepting quarterly payments from Prestige Builders is the same as receiving charity."

"Convince her otherwise," Steve suggested matter-of-factly.

"Easy for you to say," Linc countered. "You've had an entire year to accomplish the feat, however, and haven't managed to pull it off."

"But then I was never as close to Erin as you were."

Linc's gaze shot to his brother. He read no censure in Steve's neutral expression. For the first time, Linc wondered how successful he'd been in concealing his attraction to Erin from his older brother.

"Of course, she's probably upset with you for skipping out on her after Merrill's death," Steve continued reflectively.

"Yeah, you could say that."

"The way around that would be for you to spend some time with her before the Wednesday meeting—take her out to dinner, maybe dancing."

Linc stared at his brother as if he'd lost his mind. *"Dancing?"*

Steve nodded. "Sure, why not?"

*Because if I hold her in my arms, I'm not sure I can let her go without making love to her.*

Before Linc could come up with an acceptable answer, the phone rang. Steve reached over and picked it up.

"Steve Severance here." There was a brief pause. "Terrance, I appreciate you returning my call. I know it's a pain, meeting on Sunday, but my brother and I would appreciate you dropping by the office to update us on what you've found out about those quarterly payments we discussed."

Another pause followed. Linc took the opportunity to study his brother. Steve was only eighteen months older than Linc. Throughout their teenage years a strong competitiveness had challenged their relationship. In college, however, they had managed to work through the rivalry and become friends.

"I see," Steve said into the phone. "We'd appreciate you dropping by anyway. I'd like you to speak directly with my brother."

Steve returned the phone to its cradle.

Linc leaned forward. "Well?"

"According to Terrance Jenkins, Erin appears to be in the driver's seat as to whether or not she accepts the dividend payments."

Thirty minutes later, in their meeting with the young, russet-haired attorney, Steve's observation proved prophetic. Terrance looked up from the papers he'd been sorting through, pushed his wire-rimmed glasses over his nose and closed the folder from which he'd been reading. "I don't get it. Your late founding partner's widow is *declining* her legal portion of the business's profits and you are trying to get her to *accept* them?"

"That about sums it up," Steve answered.

"But *why?*"

"Because she's entitled to it, dammit," Linc snapped.

Their attorney shook his head. "Okay, so that's why you want her to have the money. Why won't she take it?"

"Because she's too proud for her own good," Linc muttered.

"Look, I may be overstepping my bounds here, but if the woman is foolish enough not to realize what she's got coming to her, then—"

"Terrance," Steve interrupted quickly. "For your

own good, I think you'd better understand the fact that my brother and I want Erin to have the money. It's your job to see she's forced to accept it.''

The ruddy-faced attorney glanced from Steve's friendly expression to Linc, who made no effort to mask his anger with the newest associate partner at Whitsnow, LeBaron and Jenkins. Linc derived a small degree of satisfaction from watching Terrance reassess his position concerning the matter under discussion.

''Well, gentlemen, it's obvious your minds are made up,'' Terrance observed, shoving the papers he'd been handling into his briefcase. ''But there's no way you can make Erin Clay cash the checks you send her each quarter.''

''No way?'' Linc asked impatiently.

''None. Of course, the money could be set up in a trust account for your late partner's son.''

Steve got to his feet. ''That's not the solution we're looking for, but if it's the best you can do, go ahead and start the paperwork. Our tax people are nervous about having such a sizable amount of liquidity sitting on the books.''

After the attorney had left, Linc met his brother's enigmatic gaze. ''Erin needs the money now.''

Steve's eyebrows rose. ''Does she?''

''She might not need it today, but it should be at her disposal. Suppose she wants to take a trip, or go on a shopping spree or—''

''That doesn't sound much like the Erin Clay I know,'' Steve remarked casually. ''Even when she first married Merrill and had his wealth suddenly available to her, she never overspent. It was Merrill who bought the big house, the fancy cars and expensive clothes.''

The last thing Linc wanted to think about was the early days of Erin's marriage to his best friend. ''She's too thin,'' Linc muttered.

''Really? I always thought Erin had a fantastic body—tall, willowy, with just enough curves to—''

''Knock it off, big brother.'' Linc didn't bother to keep the edge from his voice.

Steve grinned. ''Why? We're discussing one sexy woman here. I mean it's not as if she were our sister or—''

Anger, raw as an exposed electrical wire, whipped through Linc. ''I know she's not our sister, but she was Merrill's wife.''

''*Was* being the operative word.'' Steve held up his hands. ''Look, I wasn't being disrespectful in any way about Erin. But I'm a man who happens to appreciate an attractive woman. Erin is single, sexy and uninvolved. Admit it, little brother, haven't you ever wondered what it would be like to take her to bed?''

Linc bit back the furious words he wanted to hurl at Steve for forcing him to think of Erin as a desirable woman when he had spent so many years repressing such thoughts.

Linc had no intention of admitting any such thing, however, not to his brother or to himself. How many nights had he laid in bed, craving the touch of her soft-skinned body against him? ''She may not be our biological sister,'' Linc replied slowly, feeling his way through the mine field of emotions churning inside him, ''but she's off-limits to us.''

Steve stared at him, his dark eyes remaining unfathomable. "And why is that?"

"Because..." At the moment Linc could think of no reasonable answer.

"I guess it really doesn't matter," Steve interrupted thoughtfully. "I'm involved with Emily now, and you're—"

"I'm what?" Linc demanded testily.

Steve tipped his head to the side. "That's right, I'd forgotten. You're footloose and fancy-free at the moment. In fact, you haven't gone out seriously with anyone in years."

Feeling unpleasantly crowded by his brother's probing questions, Linc scowled. "So what?"

"So nothing, I suppose. She's begun dating again, you know."

"Erin?"

"That's who we're talking about," Steve drawled.

"She's too vulnerable to go out in the world."

"Perhaps." Steve draped one leg casually over the other. "Have you considered how you're going to feel when Erin finally gets over Merrill's death and falls in love with someone else?"

Linc felt as if a fist had plowed into his gut. "She's barely begun dating again."

"Yeah, but we've already established the fact that she's one sexy woman. She's also young and beautiful and rich—just the right combination to bring the eligible and maybe not-so-eligible men pouring out of the bushes. *And* she's a widow."

"Meaning?"

"Meaning she's got all those unmet physical needs clamoring to be satisfied with no after-divorce bitterness to work through. Face it, Linc. Erin Clay is a prime candidate for a love affair—at the very least. Yet knowing the lady, I suspect it will be a man proposing the blessed state of holy matrimony who finally snares her."

Linc remembered how Erin had looked with her face tilted toward his and her parted lips a scant inch from his. His palms began to sweat.

"And," Steve continued, "because of your noble little cover-up regarding the circumstances surrounding Merrill's death, Erin has no idea her late husband isn't worth a thimbleful of grief."

"You would have done the same," Linc said through gritted teeth.

Steve shrugged. "Maybe. At the end, I was pretty fed up with Merrill's antics. I might have decided it was better for Erin to discover the truth about the man she'd married."

"It would have devastated her."

"She would have recovered," Steve countered mildly.

"Why put her through the additional grief?" Linc challenged.

His brother's dark eyes held Linc's. "None of us can play God with other people's lives, Linc. Sooner or later the truth will come out, and Erin will have to deal with it."

"It's been over a year," Linc pointed out.

"So it has." His brother stood and moved to the door. "Give my regrets to Erin's father tonight."

"You mean you're not coming to his farewell party?"

"I'd like to, but I'll be leaving town right after our

meeting on Wednesday, and I have some loose ends to tie up before then.''

"How long will you be gone?" Linc asked, caught off guard by Steve's announcement. "I've got to get back to the L.A. office."

"Actually you don't." Steve stretched lazily. "It's been years since I've taken a vacation, and I've decided to take one in southern California. Don't worry about the L.A. branch—I'll look in on things there."

Linc eyed his brother's relaxed pose through narrowed eyes. "Who's going to be running things here?"

A slow grin eased across Steve's face. "Kind of convenient you being in town, isn't it?"

"When did you decide you needed a vacation?"

"I had my bags packed the minute your plane touched down on the runway, little brother."

"How long is this vacation going to take?"

"Well, now, that's hard to tell, but I'll be in touch."

"What about the matter of Erin's dividend checks and the end of the tax quarter coming up?"

Steve chuckled. "I guess you'll just have to get the job done yourself—whatever it takes."

Sunday night, Erin looked around her parents' family room and felt strangely alienated from the laughing, cheerful people wishing her mother and father a happy farewell. Suddenly Pulido, Mexico, sounded a million miles away.

She stood next to the patio doors that opened to the backyard and let the animated conversations drift over her. It was probably normal to be depressed by her mother and father's imminent departure. Maybe after they had left, she and Joshua would settle down to their regular routine, and she wouldn't be feeling so dislocated.

The doorbell chimed and Erin tensed. Neither of the Severance brothers had as yet made an appearance tonight, and she was more than a little jittery at coming face to face with Linc. Into her thoughts sprang the memory of the tension-charged moments when they'd stood with their gazes locked and their faces temptingly close. With that memory came a fluttery sensation she had no business feeling toward a man who clearly wanted nothing more than to have her permanently out of his life.

As if her troubled thoughts had conjured his presence, Linc walked into the family room. He stood a full head taller than her father. Both men were dressed in dark suits, but there the resemblance ended. Linc was lean and straight and endowed with whipcord tough muscles, which his hand-tailored, dark blue suit accentuated with understated yet undeniable accuracy. Her father, on the other hand, wore a vintage black suit that fit his soft physique with good-natured aplomb.

The sight of Linc slipping her father a sealed envelope forced her to remember the donations Merrill had made to her father's ministry. She didn't want to think about her late husband tonight, but she couldn't seem to help herself.

Always the question loomed on the periphery of her thoughts—had she truly loved Merrill for himself, or had it been his wealth and position in the community that had made her think she loved him? If it had been the latter, then she had done Merrill a grave disservice by marrying him. Had he paid for that disservice with his life? If they hadn't quarreled, then maybe he wouldn't have stormed out of the house that tragic night.

All at once, the room was too close, as were her memories. Knowing Joshua was tucked safely asleep in her parents' guest room and knowing she couldn't stay another minute in the packed family room, Erin stepped through the open French doors and closed them silently behind her.

The night was surprisingly sultry and the scent of her mother's carefully nurtured roses filled the air. Several gaslights provided the illumination she needed to walk along the lawn's edge toward the old, unpainted gazebo.

Grateful she had worn her sturdy, rust-colored skirt, Erin brushed aside the aspen leaves that had collected on the single bench the gazebo boasted and sat down to savor the night.

Familiar sounds ebbed and flowed around her—a few stalwart crickets, a faint breeze gently shifting newly barren branches, the distant hum of traffic. Tomorrow Joshua would start preschool, and she would begin looking in earnest for a part-time job to fill her morning hours. She knew exactly—

"So this is where you got off to."

At the sound of Linc's husky voice, Erin's eyes shot open. His arms looped casually around a weathered column, he stood outside the gazebo on its first step.

Somehow the darkness imbued him with a hint of menace. It was foolish, but her throat muscles tightened. Even as she shivered, Erin told herself she was being overimaginative. There was nothing menacing about Linc Severance. They had been friends for years.

"I needed some fresh air."

Linc looked around the deserted backyard. "You definitely found it."

What kind of reply could she make to that? Silence closed in around them.

Linc stepped into the gazebo. The floorboards creaked. "Is there room on that bench for another person?"

Good manners decreed she scoot to one side. Erin decided good manners were highly overrated. "I don't think so."

The next thing she knew he had crossed the narrow space separating them. Having no recourse, Erin made available the space he'd requested.

"I imagine on nights like tonight, you really miss Merrill," Linc said softly.

Erin sat ramrod stiff on the small bench, much more aware of Linc than she had any right to be. Again she sensed the hidden power caged beneath his dark suit. They might be friends, but it occurred to her that he had a habit of holding back while she poured out her feelings to him.

"Mostly, I was thinking about my parents leaving."

"I hadn't realized they will be flying out Friday night."

Erin brushed an invisible piece of lint from her skirt. "It's funny, but a part of me didn't think the day would really come. Dad's been talking about leaving for months, but somehow..."

Linc's strong arms gathered her to him. "You and Joshua won't be alone, you know. All your parents' friends are your friends, too."

It would have been so easy to accept Linc's comforting embrace. Instead, Erin pulled away. No more. No more would she be weak in the face of his strength.

"I don't need your shoulder to cry on, Linc."

The words were said to give herself a dose of courage. Linc's sudden intake of breath told her she'd accomplished more.

"We used to be friends," he observed quietly.

She stood. "Friends don't bail out when the going gets rough."

"I told you I had to leave."

"Right," she said, goaded by her churning emotions and the need to unburden herself. "I had become an anchor around your neck and Prestige Builders needed you in Los Angeles."

He rose, towering above her. "Is that what you think?"

She jerked her head in an affirmative nod. "It's all right, I don't blame you, Linc. Merrill never made any bones about business coming first, and he was my husband."

Linc's hands closed on her shoulders. "Oh, Erin, there's so much you don't know, so much I can't tell you."

No words he could have spoken could have angered her more. She shook herself free from a touch that was dangerously seductive and tossed the hair from her face.

"Save your breath, Linc. I've got a very clear picture about your feelings toward me."

He pushed back his coat and shoved his hands into his pockets. "Somehow I doubt that."

"Let me spell it out for you," she said softly, hugging her arms around her despite the unseasonably warm night. "You think I'm totally incapable of taking care of myself and Joshua."

He stepped closer. "Do I?"

"There's no point in denying it. Why else would you insist upon issuing me those dividend checks from Prestige Builders—unless you didn't think I could make it on my own?"

The uneven light was little help in allowing her to read his expression. From his rigid stance alone, however, she knew she'd enraged him. Good. Why should she be the only one whose nerves were frayed to the breaking point?

"What Steve and I are doing is repaying a debt to an old friend. Lord, Erin, you're Merrill's widow. You're entitled to his portion of the business."

"I'm more than Merrill's widow," she countered stubbornly. If nothing else, she was going to make sure that Linc Severance thought of her as someone other than a dead man's grief-stricken widow. "I'm an adult woman. I can stand on my own two feet. I don't need you or any man to take care of me."

"Just take the money," Linc said sharply.

A horrible sense of déjà vu struck Erin. *Just take the money.* Merrill had said those very words to her—the night he'd told her he didn't want to be married to her anymore, the night he'd told her he'd found someone else to love, the night he'd crashed into a tree going eighty miles per hour.

Erin turned from Linc, having no thought beyond escaping her damning memories and Linc's presence. She didn't make it far.

Linc's hand caught her arm and he spun her toward him. "Hey, we're not finished."

She stared at him through the blur of falling tears. "Aren't we?"

He studied her for a moment, then tugged her into his arms. This time she went. "Oh, Erin, I didn't mean to make you cry."

"You didn't, not really," she whispered against his chest. It might have made things easier if she just could have told Linc that for her to accept money from Prestige Builders emphasized as nothing else could have how deeply she had failed Merrill as a wife, as a woman.

But even on a night like this, one that invited shared confidences, Erin could not tell Linc the truth about her marriage to Merrill. She couldn't bear the thought of losing Linc's respect, and surely she would if he knew how dismally she had failed his best friend.

Linc hugged her tightly to him. The mild scratchiness of his lapel against her cheek, the satisfying weight of his arms pulling her close, the tangy scent of his after-shave—all combined to make her achingly aware that she was a woman who'd lived without a man's love for a long time. The unsteady cadence of Linc's heartbeat against her ear made her tremble.

Why hadn't she known how good it would feel to be held by Linc? Her memories of the times he'd held and comforted her after Merrill's death were hazy, and in no way prepared her for the sweetly sensual sensations tingling to life. It had been so long, too long, since she'd felt the shelter of a man's embrace.

Erin drew away from the dangerous thoughts and feelings lapping at her. The temptation, wild and fierce, to tip her face ever so slightly and press a kiss to the skin that rose just above Linc's shirt collar caught her by surprise. Her gaze dropped to the dark tie knotted at eye level. What would Linc do if she reached up and loosened—

She stepped back and stared at Linc in profound embarrassment. What was happening to her? She wasn't the kind of woman who thought about loosening men's ties and— Reluctantly, she recalled Paul's words from Friday night, that she was a woman with needs.

"I better go inside, Linc," she said hastily. *Before I do something that will make us both sorry.*

The weight of Linc's gaze checked her flight. "It's something more than the quarterly payments, isn't it?"

His voice was quiet, contemplative. Erin froze. The last thing she wanted was for Linc to discover her wayward thoughts about him. Was it possible that her excruciating awareness of Linc was some part of the grieving process? The more likely possibility that she was suffering some kind of breakdown struck her.

"It's a matter of me being in charge of my own life," she said, picking up the threads of the familiar argument.

He shook his head. "No, this is something that's going on between you and me—it has nothing to do with Prestige Builders or your quest for independence."

"There's nothing going on between us," she protested. "We're just a couple of old friends who have hit a rocky patch. When you go back to Los Angeles—"

"Which probably won't be any time soon," Linc inserted. "Steve's going to be looking after the L.A. branch for awhile."

A wave of gladness swept through Erin, catching her by surprise. She hadn't realized how much she was dreading Linc's departure. Actually, she hadn't allowed herself to think about it. "When did you decide that?"

"Steve sprang the announcement on me this afternoon at the office."

Two thoughts registered simultaneously—the decision for Linc to remain hadn't been his own, and the Severance brothers and Merrill were cut from the same workaholic cloth. Working on Sunday—they couldn't even take one full day a week from the demands of Prestige Builders. She resented keenly the hold the company had over the men who ran it.

"Your folks must be happy you've decided to stay in town for a while."

"I haven't had a chance to do more than say hello to them since I got back." Linc shifted. "This time of year they're usually packing up for the Hawaiian Aloha Festival."

Another trait Linc and Steve shared with Merrill was their lack of a close relationship with their par-

ents. Erin hadn't seen Merrill's mother and father in
over eight months, not since Joshua's last birthday.

"I really should be getting back to the house," Erin
said, feeling unaccountably sad for Linc and Steve.
Family ties were important—even when stretched by
thousands of miles.

Linc's hand came to rest on her arm. They were
close enough to the house for her to notice how
starkly his tanned skin contrasted against the white
sleeve of her silk blouse. His hold was light, light as
a velvet caress. It would have been easy to slip free
from the contact. She didn't move.

Linc's fingers began to slowly stroke her arm. She
wondered if he realized what he was doing or if the
gesture held no significance.

"At first, I thought settling the quarterly payments
was a cut-and-dried business matter."

*Like the divorce Merrill proposed to buy me off
with so he could marry his new lady love.* Erin shuddered and said nothing.

"Maybe I was being hasty," he continued reflectively. "Maybe—"

The sound of the door opening made her jump.

"Erin, are you out here?"

It was her mother's voice.

Without looking from Linc's darkened features, she
called, "Yes."

"Aunt Alyce wants to say goodbye to you, dear."

"I'll be right there."

She turned to obey her mother's summons. Linc's
hand remained in place. Erin looked over her shoulder.

She waited a half second for him to say something

further. Instead his hand dropped to his side. There were so many things that had to be said between them, yet she knew the words wouldn't be spoken tonight. As she walked to the house, she wondered if the words would ever be said.

# Chapter Five

"Mommy, I want to go *now*."

At Joshua's brightly animated expression, a poignant warmth filled Erin. "I guess it is time for us to leave."

Dressed in a kelly green shirt and slightly baggy jeans, her son straightened and marched purposefully to the kitchen door. Erin swallowed the maternal lump rising in her throat. First preschool, then kindergarten, then first grade, then... Before she knew it, she would be sending Joshua off to college.

He stood now at the back door, impatiently shifting from one short, sneaker-covered foot to another. "Hurry up, Mommy. Jake's probably already there."

Erin told herself it was ridiculous to feel betrayed by her son's eagerness to get on with his life. Sighing, she joined him at the door and reached out for his sturdy little hand. "All right, let's get this show on the road."

Outside, it was a gorgeous morning. The warming rays of the sun were already banishing the faint nip of fall lacing the air. Because the preschool was just down the street, Erin and Joshua would be able to walk to it each day, except for the coldest winter mornings.

She gave her son's hand a gentle squeeze. He looked up at her with a huge, satisfied grin. "Look, Mommy, there's Jake. We better hurry."

Erin allowed herself another sigh even as she let go of her son's hand and quickened her stride. Joshua had already reached Jake and his mother in the few moments it took for Erin to join them. The two boys immediately turned shy and retreated to their mother's sides while staring at each other with fascinated gazes.

"Are you ready for preschool?" Jake asked tentatively.

"'Course," Joshua responded with a four-year-old's bravado.

Erin smiled at Jake's mother, Teresa, a petite brunette with gentle brown eyes and a wonderful, deep laugh, which she released as she ruffled her son's hair. "Was it exciting this morning at your house, Erin?"

"Definitely," Erin answered, her gaze drifting to Teresa's inexorably widening middle and the gaily striped maternity blouse she wore. "How have you been feeling?"

Their sons quickly overcame their bout of momentary shyness and joined hands, loping up the sidewalk ahead of Teresa and Erin, who walked a few feet behind them.

"I'm feeling terrific. My morning sickness has completely disappeared."

A pang of envy touched Erin. Resolutely she suppressed it. "When Jake slept over last week, he told Joshua he was getting a little brother."

Teresa's infectious laugh burst free. Several nearby mothers also taking their children to preschool waved in Erin and Teresa's direction. The women waved back.

"We went ahead and did the test," Teresa admitted. "Bruce and our folks wanted to be surprised, but I really wanted to know if I was getting another little boy. When Jake was born, he was the first grandson on both sides of our families, and he got tons of clothes that are still just like new." Teresa shrugged. "I'm mercenary enough to want to know if I needed to repeat the process in pink."

"I can certainly understand that," Erin said, wondering if she would ever again experience the miracle of carrying a child.

"Looks like we're here," Teresa said.

Clusters of brightly dressed boys and girls stood on Diana Daxon's front lawn. Mothers were laughing and talking with one another. Diana, a tall, blond woman with dancing blue eyes and a ready smile, stood on her porch greeting the children and sending the mothers and the few fathers who'd shown up on their way.

For the most part, the boys and girls were giddy with excitement and totally indifferent to their parents' lingering, backward glances. Only a couple of children had reddening eyes and quivering bottom lips.

Joshua and Jake were not among them.

In a dishearteningly short time all the children had been rounded up and herded downstairs to Diana's basement. It would be four hours before Erin would find out how Joshua had adjusted to his first day of school.

"Well, what are you going to do with your morning?" Teresa inquired as they walked down the sidewalk.

"Start looking for a part-time job," Erin answered.

"Really?"

Erin wasn't offended by the mixture of surprise and curiosity that marked her friend's lively features. In their somewhat exclusive neighborhood, the only women who worked were those with exciting careers in medicine and law, or who taught at the university. Banebridge Drive was a place that boasted a preponderance of "mall wives," those securely married women who shopped at tasteful stores where merchandise rarely went on sale, played tennis at the club and planned exotic dinner parties.

"I think you're smart," Teresa announced after brief consideration. "It's going to be lonely for you without Joshua around."

"That's exactly what I was thinking."

"Jake had a great time when he slept over at your place last week," Teresa said, changing the subject with her customary exuberance. "It's been a month since Joshua spent the night at our place. Can he come over this Friday night?"

"I'm sure he would love to. He talked for days about the barbecue you fixed."

Teresa's booming laugh rang out again. "You

should have seen the boys up to their ears in watermelon. I let them run through the sprinklers afterward. It was the only way to get all the seeds off.''

Erin smiled. "Josh mentioned that part, too.''

Teresa stopped in front of her Victorian style home. "Then let's plan on Friday. The circus will be in town and I'm pretty sure I can get tickets.''

"Joshua would love that.''

With a casual wave, Erin said goodbye and proceeded down the walk.

When she reached her house, Erin stood on the walk and considered the dream home Merrill had built for them. She realized that she dreaded stepping into its empty interior. The house really was too large for just her and Joshua. And without Josh...

A feeling of isolation cut through Erin. One by one, the people most important to her were being taken away. Even as she accepted the fact that her grief and guilt during the past year had cut her off from the rest of the world, Erin hungered to become part of that world again. She'd already made plans and set goals to make that happen, and yet... And yet an aching loneliness tugged at her heart. Somewhere, somehow, she sensed she'd taken a wrong turn in her life and was now paying the price for it.

Critically, she examined the meticulously kept yard she and Joshua had maintained throughout the long summer. The lawn was wide and lush and green. Frost-nipped purple impatiens shaded by copper-headed marigolds bordered the sidewalk. A stand of quaking aspens curved along the edge of her property. Next to the house, tidy mums and sweet williams nodded to each other. Alongside the driveway, a young red maple, which had lavished a rich harvest of autumn leaves upon hers and the neighbors' yards, stood guard.

Erin sighed. A Utah winter was coming and in a few months all but the evergreens would stand barren. She didn't begrudge the summer's labors, however. Working outside with Josh had completed the healing process. She was stronger now than she had been, tougher, too.

The sound of an approaching vehicle penetrated her thoughts and Erin turned. A black car slowed, then pulled into her driveway. It was as if the car drifted into the drive on a current of air, unsettling the previous stillness. Several bright red maple leaves fell in a spiraling swirl before coming to rest on the lawn.

The vehicle might have been unfamiliar, but the man who opened its door and unfolded himself from its low-slung interior wasn't. Linc Severance, all six foot plus of him, stood just a few feet away. The morning sun was behind him, and Erin shadowed her eyes with her hand, squinting at him. With his dark gray suit highlighting his lean frame, he strode purposefully toward her. Erin's stomach knotted with a tension she couldn't explain or justify.

For a moment neither of them spoke. He paused, his grave features considering her as if he'd never seen her before. Self-consciously, Erin touched her hand to her cheek, realizing she hadn't put on a dab of makeup yet. She was wearing baggy jeans and a shapeless yellow sweater. Of course, none of that should have mattered to her, but somehow it did.

The silence continued to gather between them. Erin found herself so caught up in the intensity of his gaze that her mind went blank. The unrelenting honesty of the morning light mercilessly exposed the lines fanning out from Linc's eyes. There were grooves bracketing his mouth that she hadn't noticed before. But more than anything she was aware of a flash of something elementally beckoning, something elementally hungry in his gaze.

Erin had no idea how long the taut silence would have continued—until Judgment Day, perhaps. But a rogue maple leaf, freed from its moorings, drifted downward, settling upon her shoulder. Both she and Linc reached for it in the same moment.

Their hands touched. As soft skin brushed weathered skin, a jolt of electrical current seemed to arc between them. Her gaze was still trapped by his. A momentary spark flickered deep within his eyes. Her stomach curled, and she jerked her hand reflexively.

He held the crimson leaf inches from her cheek. In some still relatively sane portion of her mind, she wondered if she was dreaming this bizarre encounter.

The smallest smile hovered at the corner of his mouth. "Good morning, Erin."

She cleared her throat. "Good morning, Linc."

"Is Joshua settled at preschool?"

She nodded.

"I suppose you already had your run earlier this morning?"

She found herself fascinated by the lines and texture of his narrow lips as they shaped his unremarkable words. The morning was too warm to induce a shiver of any kind, but shiver she did. Erin told herself it was the huskiness of his voice, the slight edge of male raspiness that caused her reaction.

He still held the leaf, absently brushing its rolled edge across her cheek. She didn't know why, but the velvet scrape against her skin was almost as disturbing as the touch of their hands had been. There was nothing to do but back away a step and square her shoulders.

Linc looked at the leaf he held, and his eyes widened as if he was surprised to find himself gripping the gaudy thing. Beneath his expensively-tailored suit, she sensed his tension. His fingers released the leaf and a sudden breeze captured and lifted it, making it dance just inches above their heads. Then, capriciously, the wind dashed it to the lawn where it joined the rising cluster of other autumn casualties.

"Why are you here?" Erin asked, forcing her gaze to return to his.

He shoved his suit coat back and, in a familiar gesture, jammed his hands into his pockets. Abruptly, it occurred to Erin that Linc Severance was nervous. Disbelievingly, she rolled the thought around in her head. It didn't seem likely. After all, implacable men didn't get nervous, did they?

"I'm not here to argue," he said at last, as if the words had been wrung from him.

She shook her head, trying to make sense of the awkard tension that continued to pulse between them. It was daylight and she wasn't dreaming. Linc was Linc, and she was herself, and none of this made a lick of sense. The rising wind tugged at his neatly combed hair. A black lock fell across his forehead and Erin experienced the strongest temptation to brush it into place.

More leaves blew around them. As they stood facing each other, Erin had the oddest feeling that Linc needed some kind of reassurance from her. "Come inside."

Even as the words escaped her lips, she wanted to call them back. It was too late, of course. Linc's hand drifted to her lower back and, in a primitively possessive gesture, he guided her to her front door. The warmth from his touch seeped easily through the thin barrier of her sweater. Never had she been so acutely conscious of her body, the body beneath her clothing, the body that hadn't known a man's touch in more than a year.

It was inevitable, she supposed, that one of her father's sermons should drift into her thoughts and that weakness of the flesh should be the subject of that sermon.

When the front door closed behind them, Erin stepped away from Linc. Though his gesture had been a casual one, there was nothing casual about the devious little tingles radiating through her. "Would you like some juice?"

He shook his head. "Yes."

"Yes?" she asked in confusion.

He nodded. "I mean no."

"Oh."

He tugged at his exquisite, burgundy-colored silk tie. "I'd forgotten how warm it is this time of year in Salt Lake."

It was the kind of meaningless comment that didn't require a response—not that Erin could have summoned one anyway. She really wasn't interested in small talk. Pretty sure that she knew his motive for stopping by, Erin wanted the meeting over with. Her

mind was made up about the quarterly payments
and—

"Steve thinks we should spend some time together
before the Wednesday meeting."

Linc's stark announcement shattered her train of
thought with the explosiveness of a time bomb going
off. "What?"

"He thinks that will help me understand why you
feel the way you do about Merrill's share of the business."

It was ridiculous, but Erin felt as if she'd been
slapped. "Is that why you came back from Los Angeles? Because your older brother told you to?"

"Actually, it was our attorney," Linc clarified.

"If they told you to jump off a building, would
you?"

Linc blinked. "What?"

"Oh, never mind." She stalked to the kitchen.
There were dishes to do and several shops she wanted
to visit before noon. Her schedule was much too
crowded for her to accommodate making a fool of
herself.

She reached the doorway leading to the kitchen
when Linc's arm descended across it like a falling
rail-crossing guard.

"What's gotten into you, Erin? You're as prickly
as a..."

*You've gotten into me,* she wanted to shout at the
irritating man. Failing that, she would have loved to
have told him it was PMS—just to shake him up. But
the truth was he already seemed sufficiently shaken.

With a start Erin realized he'd stopped speaking
and they were staring at each other again—deeply.

She couldn't be sure, of course, but it seemed as if their breaths rose and fell in identical rhythms.

His unyielding arm continued to rest across the swell of her breasts, blocking her path, holding her in some kind of emotional and physical gridlock from which there seemed no escape.

His lips parted. She waited for him to say the words that would release them from their strange paralysis.

"Oh, Erin..."

Those weren't the words.

"Linc?"

And there was the rational part of her brain choosing to kick into gear, reminding her that only two days earlier Linc and she had stood on the other side of this very door and almost... Her mind wouldn't deliver the word, but her heart was more generous.

She tilted her face toward him. She had to know, had to know how it felt to have his mouth on hers. Just once, she told herself. If he would kiss her just once as a man kisses a woman, then all the awkwardness between them would end.

"Please..." She spoke the word or, more accurately, she breathed the whisper. And what an insignificant whisper it was. Just an exhalation of breath, holding a plea to end the torment.

His head lowered.

Erin sucked in as deep a breath as she could hold with so little warning. She knew she was going to need it, because she had no intention of coming up for air until—

He took his time closing the distance between them. She resisted the urge to grab hold of his tie and force him to complete the impending contact, to end the agony of anticipation.

"Fair warning, Erin," he growled, his mouth a heartbeat away. "Run if you're going to."

*Run?* How little he knew her, or the hot yearnings rising within her.

"Kiss me, damn you."

Incredibly, he smiled. Their lips touched. His fingers gripped her shoulders and, with a violent tug that made her stomach flip over, he pulled her to him.

The kiss began.

It was football season, so why should she have been surprised at being blindsided? But there she was, standing in the hallway between the kitchen and living room, feeling as if she'd been tackled by a three-hundred-pound something or other and knocked breathless, brainless and boneless. Luckily, there was no pain involved.

Only pleasure.

The kind of hot, licking pleasure that made her press herself against the solid length of him. The kind of pleasure that made her part her lips and invite his tongue inside. The kind of pleasure that made her burn and writhe and wind her fingers through the silky swath of his hair.

Her eyes were closed and she saw every color in the rainbow, plus a few she hadn't known existed. She might have moaned. Erin wasn't sure. Someone did, and there were only the two of them in the house.

The kiss had begun tempestuously, almost savagely, but inexorably the mood changed as Linc's mouth gentled against hers, allowing the intimacy to become even deeper. She tasted him. He tasted her.

Even as she wanted to savor the moment, to prolong it, Erin felt him begin to pull away.

It had to end sometime, of course. Erin discovered there was pain, after all. But it came from the parting, not the joining.

Finding a measure of courage she hadn't known she would ever have to dig for, Erin opened her eyes and encountered Linc's steely gaze. *What does it mean?* She wanted to ask, but refrained. Linc's eyes held pain. She sensed that for him the pain came not from the separating but from the temporary madness that had seized them.

In that moment, Erin knew she'd recovered from Merrill's betrayal. She knew because she wouldn't have felt Linc's withdrawal so keenly if she'd still been locked inside the emotional vacuum that had imprisoned her for the past year.

She looked deeply into Linc's eyes, needing to understand his feelings at this moment. His gaze held only regret. Coldness squeezed her heart. "I—I think you'd better leave."

"I didn't plan for this to happen," he said, as if excusing the kiss, the insanity and the passion.

Erin didn't want what had happened between them excused away as if it was an embarrassing hiccup. "You don't have to apologize," she said, digging for composure. "Things like this happen all the time."

His features loomed hostile above her. "Look, what just happened was a mistake, pure and simple."

She straightened. "Obviously."

He turned to leave, then paused. "The best thing we can do is forget it."

"I agree."

His scowl became more ominous. "Then you accept my apology?"

Erin's control snapped. "Let me give you a tip for future reference, Mr. Severance. The last thing a woman wants after a kiss like that is an apology."

"What does a woman want after a kiss like that?" he asked, his tone mocking.

"Flowers," Erin answered, spurred by a burr of anger that refused to die meekly. "Or maybe chocolate, or a fancy greeting card, or an invitation to bed. Or anything the world has to offer—*except* an apology. Got that?"

A flame flickered in the depths of his eyes. "An invitation to bed?"

His low voice stroked every female nerve she possessed. He would of course seize upon that ill-chosen remark.

With more pluck than valor, Erin raised her chin and met his smoldering gaze head on. "I believe that's the general chain of progression."

"I'm going to hate myself for this, but I've got to know. How many times since Merrill's death have you followed that...chain of progression?"

"Just once," she answered softly, "but he was too big a fool to figure it out."

With that parting pearl of wisdom, she opened her front door and proceeded to push Linc through it. He didn't go. Damn, she hated it when a man missed his exit line.

"Erin?"

Sunlight and wind poured through the open doorway. "Yes?"

"Was I that man?"

She looked up into his rugged, heart-stoppingly masculine features and had to fight the temptation to shake him silly. Only one thing stopped her. Erin knew he wouldn't let her get away with it.

She shoved the hair from her face and settled for glaring at him. "Perhaps, for a brief moment."

As far as she was concerned it was more of an explanation than he deserved.

"And the moment's over?"

Along with Linc's clearly evident chagrin, a sparkle of mischief shone in his eyes. Her gaze narrowed. That he could find *anything* about this situation even the least bit amusing fired her hair-trigger temper— the hair-trigger temper that until now she hadn't known she possessed.

"I agree. It's best forgotten." *No, you don't!* a little demon shouted from within.

He rubbed his jaw, his gaze returning to her mouth. She licked her lips and wondered if he might possibly kiss her again—this time without the regrets.

"About that invitation to bed..." he continued, his voice low.

"Yes?"

"Better be careful to whom you extend it. The next guy might not be so noble."

Linc was gone before Erin could vent the raw, feminine rage that whipped through her. She settled for slamming the door. It was a paltry release for her pent-up anger, but short of stomping her foot—which she refused to let him reduce her to—it had to suffice.

Erin showered and dressed quickly, then made her rounds at several nearby shops. She knew most of the women who worked in them, knew they worked for minimum wage, and yet that knowledge didn't discourage her. Erin had sufficient money in the bank to live comfortably on the interest if she so chose. She didn't. Maybe later her plans would change, but for now she was interested in working part-time.

A bell tinkled as she entered the third craft store she'd visited that morning. Its proprietor, Velma, a wide redhead in a gaily printed muumuu, looked up from the orange pom-poms she was separating by size. "Good morning, Erin. Are you looking for something new for Halloween this year?"

Erin glanced at the glass counter covered with goofy, good-natured ghosts, smiling beak-nosed witches and roly-poly pumpkins sporting sappy grins. Josh would love them. He was so excited about going trick-or-treating this year. Even though the holiday was more than a month away, he already knew what he wanted to be—a Smurf.

"These are adorable," Erin said, picking up a homely witch with a spider dangling from her pointed chin.

"And a snap to make," Velma said.

"I'm definitely interested, but that isn't the reason I stopped by this morning."

"No?"

"I was wondering if perhaps you had a position opening up for part-time help?"

Velma's round face filled with surprise. "You mean for yourself?"

"I'm looking for something to do in the mornings while Joshua's at preschool."

"I do have a job coming available in November,

but the pay isn't very much." The shopkeeper studied Erin dubiously.

Erin couldn't help smiling. She had received the same reaction from two other store owners. "The pay really isn't that important to me, Velma. You know how I'm always immersed in some project or another. I just thought I'd enjoy working in a place like this while Josh is in school."

Velma's features cleared. "You're probably my best customer. It wouldn't be good for business for me to turn you down."

"Is that a yes?"

The woman smiled broadly. "If you're looking for morning hours, it's a definite yes."

Erin set down the witch. A feeling of triumph washed through her. She'd taken another step in getting into the mainstream. Oh, she knew how tiny a step it was. But it was a beginning.

She reached for a tiny silk pumpkin. "Do these come in a kit, Velma?"

"They sure do. Here, let me show you the scarecrow and bat that come with the set."

The rest of the morning passed quickly. Erin thought of Joshua only forty or fifty times, wondering how he was adjusting to Diana's preschool. Of course, with his best friend, Jake, by his side, she was pretty sure her son was in fine spirits.

Minutes after leaving Velma's shop, Erin pulled her shiny new car to a stop in front of Diana's house. Other mothers were clustered in the large yard, chatting with one another. Smaller children played tag in the fall leaves that lay in accommodating heaps beneath their dancing, sneakered feet.

Erin turned off the engine and stared at the wonderfully American scene before her. For no reason at all, she thought of Linc, something she'd done her best to avoid all morning. Unwillingly, her fingertips left the steering wheel and touched her lips. She could still feel him, not just the relentless pressure of his mouth against hers, but the length and breadth of him as he'd held her in his arms.

A lazy heat began to grow within her. She'd wanted more. She could admit that to herself as she sat alone in the car. More of the kissing and a lot more of the touching. How would it feel for his bare skin to brush up against hers? How would it feel to run her fingertips across the dark hair that covered his chest? How would it feel to lay in a bed with him, to give herself utterly and completely to Linc Severance?

Shakily Erin dropped her hand to the steering wheel and opened the car door. Never in her life had she experienced such wanton thoughts, thoughts that were at odds with the conservative way she'd been raised. She sighed. Did it really matter what Linc had made her feel when he'd taken her into his arms?

It was as clear as the Utah sun shining down on her that Linc Severance was determined to fight the attraction that had sprung up between them. If Erin didn't want her heart broken, she would be wise to adopt that same indifferent attitude. Obviously Linc regretted the moment of madness that had raged out of control between them.

Erin trudged through ankle-deep leaves up the front walk. Why *had* he kissed her? Simple curiosity? They had been friends for years. Had he just wanted to see what it felt like to hold her in his arms? Well, she hoped he was satisfied—because he'd stirred up a host of wicked desires within her.

*Why did you kiss him?*

The question came from nowhere, and Erin chose to ignore it for now.

Diana's front door opened and a short but energetic line of eager, giggling children formed behind Diana's arm. Erin moved closer with the other adults as Diana released the children one by one to their waiting parents.

Not surprisingly Josh and Jake stood next to each other.

Teresa's booming laugh rang out. "Well, hello there, stranger."

Jake bounded into her arms. "It was great, Mom. We made touchie feelies. See?"

Joshua came out behind his friend, waving a strangely decorated paper plate. "Lookit what we did, Mommy."

Erin ruffled her son's hair and automatically reached for the plate being shoved toward her with youthful exuberance. "Wow."

"Isn't it great?" Joshua demanded excitedly.

A closer look at the plate showed that various items had been glued to it—a scrap of sandpaper, a piece of velvet ribbon, a straight pin, some pine cone petals and a cotton ball.

"It's spectacular," Erin agreed.

Joshua smiled in satisfaction. "I know, and I made it all by myself—with *paste*," he added importantly.

"I'd say you did a great job. Let's celebrate."

His brown eyes sparkled at her. "Cel'brate, how?"

"With a hamburger and french fries," she answered, naming Joshua's two favorite foods.

"Can I get a kiddie meal?" he asked immediately.

"On a day like today, you bet," she said, squeezing his hand.

"All right!"

They walked toward her car with Joshua making a show of tugging on her hand to hurry her up.

Erin was smiling at him when a shadow passed between them and the sun. She looked up, and the smile died.

Linc was back. Again. He stood at the end of the walk with his hands jammed in his pockets and his sober eyes taking in her and Joshua. For just a moment Erin thought she glimpsed an aching loneliness in those watchful eyes of his. *Was* he lonely? Then in the space of a blink his expression became shuttered, and she was left wondering if she'd only imagined his melancholy.

"Where are you headed?" he asked in that damnably calm voice of his, as if he hadn't hours ago kissed her within an inch of ecstasy.

"To get hamburgers and french fries," Joshua announced grandly.

"Sounds good." Linc turned in the direction of her house. "I'll drive."

Erin opened the passenger door of her car and let Joshua inside. "That's all right, I'll drive."

Linc's head whipped around, and she felt his stare on her as she fastened Josh's seatbelt. Naturally her hands trembled, but she still managed to get the job done in a respectable space of time.

"This is *your* car?" Linc demanded in obvious astonishment.

"I bought it a couple of weeks ago. What do you think?"

She was already reaching into her purse for the keys. The way she figured it, the odds were in her favor that she and Joshua could escape without Linc joining them. No matter how hard she stretched her imagination, Erin could not visualize the debonair Linc Severance inside a fast-food restaurant.

Linc's gaze moved slowly across the glossy exterior. "It's red."

"I like red." She hated the defensive tone in her voice.

"It's a convertible."

He pronounced the word with the same degree of disapproval he might have voiced had she double-parked an alien spacecraft in front of Diana's house.

Erin moved steadily around the car to the driver's side. "I happen to like convertibles."

"You bought a red convertible," Linc said slowly as if needing to hear the words aloud.

"You bet I did," Erin said more to herself than him. With no fanfare, she opened the car door and slipped inside. Immediately she inserted the key and turned on the ignition.

There was no squealing getaway, however. As if he'd been doing so for years, Linc calmly got into the back and casually fastened his seatbelt.

"Lady, you're just full of surprises."

He muttered the observation under his breath but Erin heard him, and his words echoed in her mind all the way to the golden arches.

## Chapter Six

Erin had been right. Linc in a fast-food restaurant was definitely not the stuff of reality. Perhaps it was his custom-tailored suit, or perhaps it was his silk tie and expensive leather loafers, or perhaps it was his resigned manner as he bit into a double cheeseburger that convinced Erin Linc Severance didn't often dine in establishments sporting vinyl booths and simulated wood tables.

Linc chewed thoughtfully for a moment, then wiped his mouth with a napkin. "Shouldn't this place be off-limits for a health nut?"

Rebelliously, Erin poked a French fry into her mouth and took her own sweet time about answering. "I'm not a health nut, nor am I a fanatic."

"Mommy, show him your touchie feelie," Joshua urged as he snared the pickle from his burger and popped it into his mouth.

"I left it in the car," she answered absently as she

picked up her drink. The soda made it up the straw but not down her throat as she caught the sudden gleam in Linc's eyes.

She coughed a full minute and her eyes were watering when she finally stopped. She took another sip of soda to soothe her throat. "At preschool today, the children decorated paper plates with different textured materials. Their teacher calls it a touchie feelie."

Linc's gaze was smack dab on her mouth. Erin resisted the urge to lick her lips. Not by word or deed did she intend to fuel Linc Severance's awareness of her as a woman, not when that awareness so obviously repelled him.

"Makes sense," he answered finally, wrapping his mouth around another bite of his burger.

Erin scowled at him, wondering why on earth he'd joined them. It infuriated and alarmed her that she was unable to understand either him or his actions since he'd returned to Salt Lake. She nibbled another fry. It occurred to her that, even though she'd thought of Linc as a friend for years, there was a significant part of himself he'd always kept private.

As she reflected upon it, Linc Severance had been there more for her than she had for him. He had done the listening. She had done most of the talking. That discovery was strangely unnerving, along with the memory of the personal things he had done for her immediately following Merrill's death.

She took another sip of her drink and listened as Linc read the riddles off the kiddie meal box to Joshua. As she watched him, Erin had the feeling that until now, Linc had been like a dark horse in her life, circling the perimeter of her world but never truly being a part of it or allowing her the opportunity of being a part of his.

Then in the space of three days he'd impacted her structured life like a comet streaking through the heavens. In many ways his manner still closed her out, yet he was continually forcing *her* to open up to him. She wouldn't deny that there was a strength and intensity to him that intimidated her. He was so much stronger than she was, both physically and in some other way she couldn't define. Linc had defenses and barriers she could only begin to guess at.

Erin realized she was sensing these hidden facets to Linc's character now because she was more aware of him as a man, as a person, than she had been before.

*Strip away those defenses. Break down those barriers.*

The demon thought spiraled through her reflections, leaving Erin shaken and more fiercely conscious of Linc, of his undeniable masculinity, than she wanted to be.

What would it take for him to kiss her again? What would it take for him to make love to her? What would it take for him to fall in love with her?

Horrified by the unfamiliar direction of her thoughts, Erin's hands closed into fists in her lap under the table. What was happening to her? She had been raised by conservative parents, she had known only one man physically in her entire life, and now she was suddenly harboring lustful thoughts about a man who'd been her friend for years.

None of it made any sense. And she didn't want it to. She wasn't ready to face this new side of her nature, a side she hadn't known existed and felt woefully inadequate to explore. But as she assessed Linc's laughing face while he read the answer to yet another ridiculous riddle to her son, something quickened within her, and Erin realized that it was frighteningly easy for a woman to keep secrets from herself. The kind of secrets that could plunge the woman into deep waters, waters so deep that even an excellent swimmer such as herself might find it impossible to stay afloat.

When they left the restaurant, Erin was still grappling with an awareness of Linc that was almost abrasive. During the drive home, she found herself wondering about his social life, about whom he might be currently dating...or sleeping with.

Every time she glanced into her rearview mirror, she met his contemplative expression. Again she wondered about his thoughts, wondered about the soul-wrenching kiss he'd unleashed, wondered about his frightening capacity to affect her so profoundly upon so many different levels.

As they pulled into her driveway, Erin noticed his car parked in front of her house. With Joshua present as a buffer between them, she should have felt secure and better able to deal with Linc. Her sigh was lost to the rising wind as she stepped from her car. She felt about as secure as the maple leaves currently swirling around them.

Both she and Linc reached Joshua's side of the car at the same time. Linc stood back while she unbuckled the seat belt. In a burst of boyish delight Joshua's small legs propelled him through the leaves that had collected upon their lawn.

Erin tossed back her hair, her laughter joining her son's. She couldn't resist chasing after him. Maybe she was grasping at straws to release the tension that seemed to coil within her whenever Linc was present. She wrestled Joshua to the ground. Tickling seemed the most logical course of action. Josh squealed, then squirmed free. The next thing Erin knew her adorable son was heaping armfuls of leaves on top of her. In self-defense, she scooped up a handful and let go of her own crimson volley.

Joshua danced just out of range. "Can't catch me, Mommy."

Erin got to her feet and shook off the mountain of leaves. "Oh, yes, I can."

She never knew when Linc joined their ragtag game, but soon both he and Joshua were attacking her with mounds of flying leaves. Breathless, seconds away from ridiculous giggles, Erin held up her hands in surrender.

"It's two against one—that's not fair!"

Joshua lunged forward. His short but surprisingly strong little arms anchored her knees. "I got you, Mommy!"

There was no way to keep her balance. She toppled into a pile of crackling, dusty leaves and lay there for a moment before accepting the obliging hand Linc extended.

"You're covered in leaves." His voice was gruff, but there was a wonderful energy to his dark eyes that hadn't been there earlier.

Erin smiled tentatively. "You ought to look in the mirror."

Linc glanced at himself. His impeccable suit was

covered in brittle bits of crunched leaves. "I look like I've been mugged," he said with a laugh.

Which described exactly how she'd felt after his kiss, Erin reflected. She tugged at her sweater. "Let's brush off as much of this stuff as we can before we go inside."

It was only later, when he'd followed her and Joshua into her kitchen, that Erin realized she'd invited Linc inside her house. Her gaze kept drifting to the hallway door, and her hands shook as she gave Joshua the drink of water he'd requested.

After noisily guzzling his fill, Josh returned the glass to her. "I'm itchy."

"Me too, sport. Both of us need a quick bath."

She forced herself to look at Linc. His hair was mussed, his tie askew and his suit hopelessly wrinkled. He'd never looked so good.

"I was hoping we would have a chance to talk," he said in that quietly assertive way of his.

The only two things they had to talk about were the dividend payments and the kiss they'd shared, neither of which she cared to discuss. "I think we've pretty much said everything there is to say."

He shook his head. "Not from where I'm standing."

"Mommy, I'm *really* itchy."

Erin glanced at her son. With supreme indifference to society's strictures, he was energetically scratching his privates. The hot blush that crawled to her cheeks was more embarrassing than her son's actions.

"Uh, okay, a bath it is."

"I'll be waiting for you."

Erin glared at Linc. She hated it when he used that macho tone with her. "Suit yourself."

She marched Joshua up the stairs without a backward glance and ran her son through a thorough bathing, which included shampooing his short, dark hair. It was well past Joshua's usual nap time, and she didn't have any difficulty getting him to fall asleep.

When that task was completed, she headed for her own bathroom and a lengthy shower. With a head full of shampoo, she cussed Linc's stubborn reappearance in her life. Why wasn't he at the office? She knew he was just as much a workaholic as Merrill had been. It made no sense for him to hound her about the wretched checks, either. Good grief, whoever heard of a corporation trying to *give* its money away?

It was when Erin was towel drying her hair that she began to seriously wonder if she had the nerve necessary to walk downstairs and talk to Linc for the third time in a single day. She gazed at her steamy reflection in the mirror. The contrast of her dark eyebrows against her skin and her too-generous mouth were her most noticeable features.

*Okay, Erin, what next?*

*I'll get dressed, go downstairs and show Linc Severance out the door. Perhaps this time he'll stay out.*

*But you want him to stay in....*

Erin turned from her reflection.

He was sorry about the damned kiss.

That said it all. Well, not quite. *She* wasn't the least bit sorry, she realized. It had been a glorious kiss, a spectacular kiss, the kind of kiss Hollywood plastered across giant billboards to sell theater tickets.

With more haste than grace, Erin pulled on clothing

appropriate to show a man how indifferent she was to him. A comfortable pair of jeans, a baggy sweatshirt sporting a university logo and *no* makeup. That certainly made a statement.

She padded down the stairs barefoot and pushed open the door to the kitchen. It was quite empty. Keyed up for a major confrontation, Erin came to a perplexed halt. Damn, she couldn't figure him out. What was he up to?

Later that afternoon, Erin stared at the last great zucchini her garden had produced. She'd already made everything from the other zucchinis she'd grown this summer that she cared to, as well as given away as many as she dared. This time of year people tended to look unkindly upon the prolific vegetable.

Erin hated throwing them away. In that way, she was like her mother, she supposed. From habit her hand stretched toward the kitchen phone. It took a moment for her to remember that her mother was no doubt in a packing frenzy and wouldn't appreciate the interruption. In just four short days, her parents would be flying to Mexico. Erin's hand dropped.

She frowned at the zucchini. Afraid of the real possibility she might pick it up and throw it through a window, she left the kitchen in search of Joshua. It wasn't much of a search. He was in the family room playing with a menagerie of plastic farm animals.

When she stepped into the room, he was lying on his stomach nose to nose with a pink pig.

"Can pigs fly, Mommy?"

"No, sweetheart," she answered, picking up several of the storybooks scattered around.

"How come people say when pigs fly, then?"

Erin sat in an easy chair and smiled. "That's just a different way of saying never."

Josh was silent for a moment. "If pigs had wings, could they fly?"

"I suppose so."

"If I had wings, could *I* fly?"

"Absolutely," Erin answered.

Her son rolled onto his back and gazed at her from an upside down position. "Then can my daddy fly 'cause he's an angel?"

Erin's smile faltered. She hadn't seen this coming. "Hmm, I wouldn't be surprised."

For several minutes, Josh's face was scrunched in deep thought. "When I die, I want propellers. They're faster."

At Joshua's careless words, Erin's heart constricted. Just the thought of her son... She closed her eyes. She couldn't think about it, or she'd never let him out of the house again.

"You're not going to die, honey," she said firmly.

Joshua sat up, pig in hand. "Grandma and Grandpa are the next ones to die, 'cause they're the oldest," he pronounced sagely.

Erin's heart took another painful lurch. She didn't believe in premonitions. She refused to. "No one's going to die."

"Good," Joshua said cheerfully. "I don't want to be put in a box under the ground."

She hated to, but Erin had to ask. "What brought all this up?"

"Jenny's new kitty got runned over, and they put it in a box in the backyard and buried it."

"I see."

"She brought Bouncer's collar to preschool and told us all about it."

"Bouncer was the kitty?"

"Yeah." Joshua nodded, dropping the pig and walking to her. "Then Brian told everybody that his grandpa died 'cause he got so old and that *everybody* was going to die sometime." Josh crawled on her lap and stared at her earnestly. "I don't want to die, Mommy—even if I do get a propeller."

Erin hugged him close and didn't even try to hold back the tears. "No one's going to die," she repeated staunchly. "Not for a long, long time."

Joshua peered at her. "Why are you crying, Mommy?"

"I—I just got something in my eye."

Her son's gaze dropped to the books stacked nearby. "Read me a story."

When his thumb wandered into his mouth, Erin didn't say anything. She sank back on the chair and opened up one of his favorite books, the one about finding the hat that fit just right.

In a few moments, she noticed the thumb was no longer providing sustenance. She nestled her chin against Joshua's head and read softly. There was no way to suppress the burst of maternal pride she experienced when Joshua began repeating many of the words from memory. Probably all mothers thought their children were geniuses. But Erin was convinced Josh was an exceptional child.

The ringing of the doorbell curtailed images of him taking the presidential oath.

When Erin opened the front door and saw Linc

Severance staring at her, she felt as if she'd stepped into the Twilight Zone. Four times in one day. It had to be a record. Then her gaze took in what he was wearing—snug jeans and a navy blue T-shirt. She sucked in her breath. He looked good, real good.

She noticed the heavy, professional-looking toolbox he carried and her brow furled. "Uh, Linc, what are you doing here?"

It was a logical question, after all. She didn't understand his sudden scowl when she asked it.

"I came to fix the dishwasher and make a final pitch for you to reconsider—"

"Yeah!" Joshua cheered, interrupting what Erin knew was Linc's main purpose for showing up. "Can I help?"

"You can be my right-hand man," Linc answered, moving forward.

Erin had a choice—to step aside or be mowed down. She closed the door and leaned against it. It occurred to her that she still didn't have on a bit of makeup and, while that had been her intention earlier, she suddenly didn't want to look dowdy around Linc. She looked longingly at the stairs. It would only take a moment for her to put on some powder and blusher. Her gaze drifted to the kitchen where ominous sounds had begun to emerge.

With a shrug, she moved in the direction of her dishwasher. Just what kind of credentials did the owner of a construction company have when it came to performing plumbing repairs?

When she stepped into the kitchen, Erin saw that Linc had already taken off the dishwasher door and removed the bottom shield. He was hunkered down freeing the plastic racks and handing them to a clearly fascinated Joshua. Something about seeing them together, intently tackling a household chore like father and son, made Erin's heart beat faster.

*I don't want you here!*

She wanted to shout at Linc. In the few short days he'd been in Salt Lake he'd forced her to think and feel things she wasn't ready to confront. Seeing him with her son, the most precious and important part of her life, shook Erin. Because seeing them together reminded her of the lack of a man in Joshua's life.

Somewhere along the line she'd convinced herself that Josh really didn't need a father, not if Erin was a good enough mother, anyway. In the space of a few minutes, however, it had become terrifyingly clear to her that Joshua was vulnerable in that area of his life. Her son did need a father. Erin sagged against the wall, staring at Linc and Josh as they proceeded to deftly dismantle the dishwasher's innards. And a father was one thing she couldn't go out and buy her son—at any price.

"Got any newspaper, Erin? I hate to dirty up your floor."

Joshua bolted to his feet. "I'll get it."

Linc's gazed followed the boy, then lifted to the boy's mother. Why was Erin so pale? She looked as if someone had shot her pet puppy. All he was doing was trying to help her—first with the dishwasher, then with the dividend checks. After that, he'd be out of her life again, this time for good.

He figured it was like surviving a trial by fire. Once the flames were extinguished, he would always carry the scars, but at least his attraction to her would be burned away. And this time they wouldn't part enemies.

"Great kid," Linc said, needing to break the uneasy silence.

"Yes, he is."

*And I want to take his mother to bed and make love to her until neither one of us can move.* Linc swore softly under his breath. Dammit, he was putting those thoughts behind him. She needed a friend, and he was going to be that friend during the short time he remained in Salt Lake. Surely he had enough discipline and character to help her out without giving in to his baser instincts, especially since he was on his way to crushing the attraction he felt toward her once and for all.

Joshua returned with the newspapers, and Linc extracted the clogged filter from Erin's dishwasher. It took only a bit of patience to clean the device. Of course, with Joshua's help the process took an hour longer than it should have, but Linc couldn't regret the extra time with the bright-eyed boy.

Finally, the job was done, except for replacing the pump, which was showing a lot of wear. He assumed Erin would want Mr. Lucco to handle that repair. As Linc put away his tools, his gaze fell upon something huge and green on Erin's counter. "What's that?"

"Zoobikini," Joshua answered. "Mommy makes all kinds of stuff from it."

"What kind of stuff?" Linc asked skeptically. It didn't look like anything he'd want to eat.

"Like zoobikini bread and zoobikini jam."

Linc shuddered. "It looks like some kind of squash."

Erin bestowed a suspiciously brilliant smile upon him. "It is, Linc. Would you like to have it?"

He backed away. "What for?"

"For fixing the dishwasher."

"I meant what would I do with it?"

"Use it as a doorstop?" she inquired sweetly.

He wanted to jerk her into his arms and kiss her smart mouth into submission. When he encountered Joshua's earnest young face, Linc felt like the lowest kind of pervert.

"I think I'll pass."

"All right."

"Can you stay for dinner?" Joshua asked suddenly in the sublimely innocent manner kids have of issuing such invitations.

"That's up to your mother."

Joshua turned to her. "Can he, Mommy? Can he?"

Erin frowned at both of the men in her kitchen. There was no tactful way to send Linc on his way. After all, he *had* fixed the dishwasher. "Of course, he can stay," Erin said, answering Josh instead of Linc.

Joshua stared at her with wide, curious eyes. "What're we having?"

"I'll warm up the leftover stew."

"With biscuits?" Joshua asked hopefully.

"With biscuits," Erin answered.

Josh clapped his hands. "You'll love Mommy's biscuits. They're the bestest."

"I'm sure they are."

Erin felt Linc's gaze drift slowly over her and her skin heated. He had that special way of looking at her that made her heart race and her stomach lurch.

With a burst of activity, Erin mixed up a batch of biscuits, pulled the stew from the refrigerator to warm and tossed a quick salad. She didn't allow herself to think about Linc or his kisses or the way his jeans rode his lean body. Instead, she concentrated on not cutting off any fingers as she sliced up garden tomatoes for the salad.

In less time than she would have believed possible, she was seated at the kitchen table with Joshua and Linc. That they alarmingly resembled a family made her again uncomfortably aware that there was no man in her life she was even remotely tempted to cast in the role of father for her son. A very real part of Erin yearned to be self-sufficient. Yet another, newly awakening part of her wanted…wanted… The word "mate" drifted into her thought, and she almost groaned at the sudden longing that gripped her.

Linc and Joshua were having a meaningful conversation about spiders.

"I squished one with my shoe," Joshua confided benignly.

Linc grinned. "Did you now?"

"Uh-huh. I brought it in the house to show you, Mommy—'member?"

Even as Erin shuddered, she was grateful to have her thoughts diverted. "I remember."

Joshua's young face screwed up in a pout. "But she wouldn't take me to see that spider movie. She won't let me see the video, either."

Linc took the last bite of his third biscuit. "I guess it's pretty strong stuff, partner."

"Jake's mommy let him see it—twice."

"And Jake has nightmares," Erin said, feeling she had to defend herself.

"When he spent the night," Joshua informed Linc. "But his nightmare was about a giant toilet, not a spider."

Erin's gaze flew to Linc. He was brushing his hand over his mouth.

"I think it's time to clear the table," she said for want of anything better to say.

"And we get to use the dishwasher, right, Linc?"

"Right, partner."

It took only a few minutes to set the kitchen to rights. In those few minutes, however, Erin must have brushed up against Linc a dozen times—a dozen toe-curling, heart-stopping, spine-tingling brushes against a man she had once thought of only as a friend.

"Can we watch TV, Mommy?"

Because she needed a moment alone to collect herself, Erin sent them into the family room ahead of her. With a shaking hand, she brushed her hair from her face and stepped onto the back porch. She'd never smoked a cigarette in her life, but she imagined it was at times like this that people surrendered to the urge to fill their hands with activity and their lungs with smoke.

A widening moon filled the night sky, highlighting the looming outline of the nearby Wasatch Mountains. The wind had died down and the night was pleasantly mild. Again, Erin was tempted to swim off her excess energy. Maybe after Linc had left...

And he would leave.

She shivered and stepped inside, closing the door

quietly behind her. She wished she could call back the past, the part when she'd thought she was in love with Merrill and Linc had been her best friend.

*The time she'd thought she'd loved Merrill...*

The words mocked her. In their stark simplicity they forced her to wonder if what she'd felt toward Merrill had been merely a girlhood crush based upon his charming facade and cosmopolitan manner.

It was a damning indictment of her character that she hated accepting—just as damning as the possibility that Merrill might be alive today if she hadn't failed him. So many dark thoughts Erin had pushed to the back of her mind now crowded forward, taunting her with the futility of trying to second guess the past.

All at once, the kitchen seemed an inhospitable place, and Erin moved toward the family room where the TV was blasting an unholy ruckus. When she stepped into the room and stared at the screen, Erin couldn't believe her eyes. Two bizarrely dressed men were assaulting each other within a roped-off ring before thousands of shrieking spectators. The announcer was shouting and a giant snake was being raised above one man's head over his bloodied opponent who cowered at his feet.

"What on earth?"

"It's wrestling," Joshua explained, his eyes never leaving the screen.

Erin marched forward and turned off the TV.

"Hey!" both Joshua and Linc protested.

"I will not have my son watching this kind of violence, do you understand?" She was so angry she was shaking.

Linc rose from his chair. "Erin, I'm sorry. I didn't realize—"

"Isn't that typical," she practically shouted at him. "You didn't realize. Well, Joshua is my son and my responsibility, and I refuse to let him be contaminated by this—this…" She faltered, realizing she was making an absolute fool of herself.

"Gosh, Mommy, it wasn't that bad." Joshua sniffed.

Erin bowed her head. "Damn."

"Don't swear," Linc admonished. "It isn't good for Joshua."

*I must be losing my mind….* Erin raised her head. "I—I guess I overreacted."

"Does that mean we can turn it back on?" Joshua asked, getting to the heart of the matter.

This time Erin couldn't hold back a laugh.

"Absolutely not. Besides, it's your bedtime."

"Can Linc read me a story first?"

"I'd like that," Linc answered before Erin could veto the plea.

A shaft of pain hit her heart dead center. "If you really want to, I don't mind."

"I want to."

Erin looked into Linc's steady gaze. Some of the pain eased, but a bittersweet hollowness touched her heart when Linc sat in the same chair she had used earlier and he began reading Joshua the same story about finding just the right hat. When she saw Linc rub his jaw against the crown of Josh's head and inhale deeply, Erin's heart ached.

That night as she lay alone in her bed, Erin tried to understand the sense of floating emptiness she ex-

perienced. For the last few years she had slept by
herself. But for the first time, she was fully conscious
of that aloneness. And she wasn't thinking about
sex—well, not *just* about sex. She was thinking about
being held and doing some holding. She was thinking
about midnight whispers and shared confidences. She
was thinking about marriage—the kind she'd dreamed
of having when she'd walked down the aisle toward
Merrill.

## Chapter Seven

Wednesday morning after Erin had dropped Joshua off at preschool, she pulled into the parking lot of Prestige Builders for her dreaded meeting with the Severance brothers and their attorney.

This was the first time she'd been on the premises since Merrill's death. She stepped from her car and glanced around. Though the front office looked very much the same, the rest of the facilities had been expanded.

Noisy trucks with their gears grinding downward were pulling out of the lot. They were loaded with lumber and the other materials needed to build homes and businesses in the rapidly growing Salt Lake community. A powdery mist rose from the graveled loading area and hung in a hazy cloud above the high chain-link fence that separated the offices from the lot.

When Erin stepped into the thickly carpeted waiting room and shut the door behind her, the raucous sounds died. A young, blond receptionist dressed in a beige suit sat behind the front desk.

At Erin's entrance, the woman looked up and smiled. "May I help you?"

"I'm Mrs. Clay. I have an appointment with Linc and Steve."

The slender woman rose at once, taking a moment to smooth the lines of her suit. "The meeting's in the conference room—I'll show you where that is."

Even though Erin knew the layout of the offices as well as anyone, she allowed herself to be led through a long hallway. There was no way to keep her gaze from drifting to the office that had once been Merrill's. The door was closed, as were the others they passed.

When they reached the conference room, the young woman turned and smiled. "Steve and Linc are having a quick meeting with their attorney, Terrance Jenkins. They should be finished any minute."

Erin glanced in dismay at the long conference table covered with reams of neatly stacked materials. She had hoped the meeting would be a short one.

"Would you like something to drink—coffee or juice?"

Erin shook her head. "No, thank you."

The secretary gestured to one of the padded chairs near the head of the table. "Why don't you have a seat, and I'll let them know you've arrived?"

After the secretary excused herself, Erin began to pace. She reminded herself that she was in charge here, that there was no way she could be forced to accept money she didn't want. It was a sign of her trust in Linc and Steve that she hadn't brought her own attorney to the meeting.

A large portrait at the end of the room drew her gaze. She stopped in mid-pace. The picture was of Linc, Steve and Merrill. It had been professionally done, a gift from Mr. and Mrs. Severance when their sons and Merrill had gone into business together.

It was uncanny how the photographer had captured the very different personalities of the three young men. Linc's expression was solemn, unsmiling. Steve, on the other hand, looked quietly amused. And Merrill... Erin stared at the portrait of her late husband and waited for the twin flashes of pain and guilt. Instead she felt nothing. He was a smoothly handsome man with dark hair and playful brown eyes. His jaw held a hint of arrogance. That was all.

She reminded herself that she had made a child with the man, that he had been her first and only love. It didn't matter. She gazed at him and felt nothing. The only events she remembered with any clarity were the times he hadn't been there for her. And now firmly anchored in those gaping spaces were memories and images of Linc.

Behind her the door opened. Erin turned from the photograph. Steve entered the room first, followed by Linc and a man she assumed was their attorney.

"Erin, how are you?" Steve strode toward her and surprised her with a hearty hug. "You look fantastic."

When released from his brotherly embrace, she stepped back and grinned. "Other than a few cracked ribs, I'm fine."

Steve's eyes sparkled. "Hey, when a gorgeous woman provokes me, I react."

Erin couldn't help laughing at Steve's outrageousness. "How did I provoke you?"

He tipped his head to one side. "I guess it's the combination of your pretty face, luscious brown hair and that prim and proper gray suit, which, may I say, is covering up one delectable body."

Erin knew she was blushing. "I had to ask."

"Can we get down to business?" The question came from a scowling Linc.

"Certainly, little brother." Steve took Erin's arm and guided her toward a chair. "Here, you sit by me."

And so the meeting began, with Steve bantering and Linc looking like an angry storm cloud ready to release bolts of lightning while Terrance Jenkins straightforwardly outlined the issue under discussion. Erin forced herself to listen politely to the attorney's remarks. It was difficult to keep her expression neutral at the large sums of money he so casually mentioned. After all, as a preacher's daughter, she had been raised very frugally.

When Mr. Jenkins finished, Steve took the floor. "So you see, Erin, by the documents of incorporation and for the benefit of our accounting department, we need to get this matter resolved."

Aware of Linc's steady, unblinking gaze, Erin cleared her throat. "I understand your position, gentlemen. But I think you need to understand mine."

Linc tossed down his pen. "Erin, we *know* your position."

Steve leaned forward. "Let the lady talk."

Somehow Linc's expression became even more thunderous. "I already know what the *lady's* going to say."

"I don't," Terrance said, his plump, rosy cheeks glistening with perspiration. "And I'd very much like to understand your feelings on this, Mrs. Clay."

"I guess I feel guilty," she answered, determined to honestly state her thoughts once and for all. "Linc and Steve are doing all the work. They've already paid me back more than Merrill originally invested, and...and it just doesn't seem right."

Terrance's large, freckled hand covered hers, and Erin jumped in surprise.

"I understand what you're saying, Mrs. Clay. And I admire your integrity." He leaned forward. "May I add that your attitude is extremely refreshing in this day and age. As well as being very lovely, you are also—"

"Terrance," Steve cut in softly. "Why don't you let go of Mrs. Clay's hand and go through the waiver we asked you to draw up?"

Erin's gaze flew from the attorney's fleshy hand to Steve. Though he was slouched comfortably in his chair, his comment to Terrance Jenkins was laced with an undertone of hostility. From Steve, Erin's glance bounced to Linc. She found herself trapped in a roiling heat that raised the fine hairs on the back of her neck.

In one clumsy motion, the attorney withdrew his hand and adjusted his glasses. "Ah, yes, of course." He picked up a slim grouping of papers, cleared his throat, then began to read.

It took a moment for Erin to realize she was listening to a legal description of a sizable trust fund being set up for Joshua. A part of her wanted to be angry that she couldn't simply make the whole affair disappear. But another part was touched at Linc's and Steve's efforts to make certain that Joshua was protected financially.

When Terrance Jenkins finished reading, he laid the document aside. It was the attorney who finally broke the long moment of silence. "Well, Mrs. Clay? Have you any objection to my clients putting the trust I just read into effect?"

"Does it matter?" she asked quietly.

Linc stood abruptly. "I would like to speak to Erin alone."

The other two men also rose. Steve sauntered out, wearing an expression of satisfaction Erin couldn't begin to understand. After all, she hadn't agreed to anything at this point.

The attorney's footsteps were a little slower. At the doorway, he paused and reached into his suit pocket. "Mrs. Clay, if you have any questions, any questions at all, please call me—either at my office or at my home."

The cream-colored business card he extended never made it across the conference table to Erin. Instead, Linc intercepted it. "If Mrs. Clay, has any questions, Terrance, *I* will be the one to answer them."

Stunned by the possessive note in Linc's tone, Erin watched him usher the attorney from the room. When she and Linc were alone, he came around the table and sat in the chair Steve had vacated. "All right, let's have it."

It was a tempting suggestion. "Have what?"

"Your objections to the trust fund."

"Why did you send the others away?" She couldn't help asking. The only way she'd psyched herself up for this interview was by telling herself she wouldn't be alone with Linc Severance.

Linc leaned forward and steepled his hands over the table. "Because you were about to toss the compromise Steve and I had worked out back into our faces."

The silence of the conference room seemed a force in itself. She looked at Linc, dressed again in a somber business suit, and studied his dour expression. Was this the last time she would ever see him? Her heart twisted painfully. She didn't want their last time together to end in an argument.

"I... I wasn't going to object."

He continued to study her. "You weren't?"

She found she couldn't continue meeting his unblinking gaze and looked at her hands. They were clenched into tight fists. Deliberately, she forced herself to relax. "I know you only want what's best for Joshua—what Merrill would have wanted for his son. I've been stubborn and proud and...foolish."

The words weren't as difficult to get out as she'd thought. It was the other words trying to find their way past her constricted throat muscles that caused the pain. *Why did you kiss me? Why did you remind me that I was a woman again? Why did you invade my world and make me realize what Joshua and I were missing?*

They were questions Linc probably wouldn't have the answers to. She would never know, for she lacked the courage to ask them.

"Steve and I will take care of the legalities. There will be some papers for you to sign."

Erin nodded. She wasn't sure she could trust her voice.

"Don't be so glum," he coaxed softly. "You got your way."

Despite the moisture gathering in her eyes, she smiled sadly. "Why do you say that?"

He took her hand in his. A delicious heat moved from his callused palm through her skin and into her bloodstream. Longings, deep and unrequited, snatched the remnants of her composure.

"I wanted to make sure *you* were financially secure, Erin—not just Joshua."

She raised her gaze to his. Thoughtful and strangely turbulent, his dark eyes seemed to look into her very soul. "I am secure."

The lie was spoken in the most fragile of whispers. She felt Linc's thumb slowly stroke the suddenly sensitive flesh of her palm. "Tell me how secure you are, Erin."

If the husky taunt was meant to ruin her last shred of control, it succeeded. "I have a beautiful home that's paid for, money in the bank and a son who means the world to me."

The words came out in a shaky rush. Did Linc know what these few moments of intimacy with him were costing her? If she seriously thought he did, she probably would have strangled him.

"It's a beginning," Linc observed.

If it was a *beginning,* why was she feeling so alone? "If nothing else, Merrill was a brilliant businessman, and he left Joshua and me well taken care of."

Linc's subtle caress continued. "Will you promise me something, Erin?"

Her heart began to pound. "Promise you what?"

"That you'll let me know if there's ever anything you need?"

The keen disappointment she experienced shocked her. What had she thought he was going to ask her? She forced herself to smile reassuringly. "Don't worry about me, Linc. I'll be fine."

Somehow she had to get out of the room with her pride intact. So many alien emotions were buffeting her that she couldn't make sense of them—sorrows she had no right to feel, longings that made her body achingly aware of Linc, profound embarrassment that she couldn't control her thoughts and feelings more effectively.

"You're a babe in the woods."

It took a moment for Linc's words to sink in. Slowly, she raised her chin. Her nerves were already scraped raw and since she couldn't give vent to her softer emotions, there was always good old-fashioned anger to fall back on.

Erin stood, forcing him to let go of her hand. "What do you mean by that?"

He rose, his eyes wary. "There's no need to get on your high horse. It's just that I couldn't help noticing how Terrance Jenkins was coming on to you."

Nothing Linc said could have shocked Erin more. "Terrance Jenkins?"

"He was doing everything but drooling over you."

Unable to contain the anger building inside her, Erin frowned. "The man was merely being kind."

"Kind?" Linc snorted rudely. "The man was making an ass of himself."

"So?"

Linc's gaze narrowed menacingly. "So, you were encouraging him."

Erin's mouth fell open. "I beg your pardon?"

"You were encouraging him," Linc repeated stubbornly.

"May I ask how?"

"By being so damned beautiful," Linc all but shouted.

Erin took a step back. Linc's anger and his praise were at such odds with each other that she didn't know which to react to first.

It didn't matter. In the half second it took to close the distance between them, his hands had fastened on her arms and he was dragging her to him. For a kiss? She dearly hoped so.

But when he held her pressed against him, there was no kiss, just naked hunger blazing at her from his smoldering gaze. "What am I going to do with you?"

His question took the form of a groan. She wanted to make a suggestion, but somehow it didn't seem the right moment to say, "Take me into your arms and make me forgot what we're quarreling about."

She kept the words sealed behind pursed lips.

"I want to keep you safe," he breathed. "I want to protect you from all the garbage that's out there."

"Buy me a Doberman," she suggested, plucking

the words at random from the chaos swirling through her mind.

His gaze managed to darken further. "That's right, honey. Put the torch to the flames."

Her breath locked in her throat. "W-what?"

"I'm ready to make love to you or throttle you."

Her mind went blank, her muscles limp.

"Well?" he prompted nudging her with his hips. She felt his throbbing male hunger and almost fainted.

She licked her lips. "In either case, you'll have to lock the door first."

There was a savage flicker in his eyes. "You've got a smart mouth on you, Erin Clay."

She couldn't keep her hands from strolling up his shirt front. His neat dark tie needed loosening. She was sure of it. "Have you made up your mind?"

"About what?" he growled.

*Where to hide the body...* Was he going to make her come right out and ask him to kiss her? She stood on tiptoe and pressed herself against him. The perspiration on his brow pleased her immensely.

"You said I was a babe in the woods," she reminded him, her fingers rhythmically stroking the smooth fabric of his shirt.

His wide hands began to gently knead her arms. "Yeah?"

"Well..." She swallowed. "When you're by yourself, the woods can be a pretty lonely place."

Through her lashes, she sneaked a peek at his expression. Fascinated, she realized she was watching a war being waged—between Linc's obvious desire and his—

Deliberately, he bent his head. There was no longer

any time to try and fathom his emotions or hers. His kiss was a hot volcano caught in mid-eruption. The power of his unleashed hunger left no time for thoughts or feelings. There was only the wet fire of his possession, the steaming, fiery vortex of unappeased appetites—only Linc.

Erin felt as if she'd been set free. Never before had she experienced this intense kind of passion, which threatened to sweep her under its lavalike flow. She yielded completely. Her mouth, her hands, her body, all bent to the wild streak of desire racing through her at lightning speed. And Linc's aroused body, his hands, his mouth formed the counterpoint of her rising need.

She never knew which one of them heard the door open first. Considering the circumstances, it was amazing either of them did. But one instant they were locked in a heated embrace and the next they jumped apart, sucking oxygen into their lungs while Steve strolled into the room.

"Well, I thought the meeting went rather well, didn't you?"

Neither she nor Linc answered. They stood like dazed accident victims trying to get their bearings. Linc proved the quicker of the two to recover. "What the hell do you want?"

"To say goodbye. My plane leaves in a couple of hours for L.A. and I have some packing to do."

Linc glared at his brother. "The trip's still on?"

"Definitely." Steve turned to Erin. "Well, honey, I'm sorry your pride won't let you accept the dividend checks, but I admire your guts. You're quite a lady."

With the observation, Steve pulled her into his arms for a tight hug and kissed her lightly on the lips.

Feeling like a puppet whose strings had gotten hopelessly tangled, Erin stared at him. "Thank you."

Steve's brown eyes danced mischievously. "My brother doesn't like me holding you."

"You got that right," Linc muttered from behind them.

"But if he didn't want to be interrupted, he should have locked the door."

Erin battled the insane urge to giggle. Before she disgraced herself, Steve released her and was on his way out the door. "See you folks in a couple of months."

Erin's gaze went to Linc. He was looking at the portrait of himself, Steve and Merrill. "Damn."

Erin had the horrible feeling that if she remained in the conference room another minute, she would be treated to a second apology from Linc. In her present state of mind—or lack thereof—she didn't think she could handle that. Without saying anything, she hurried from the room. And all the way home, she told herself the kiss, the *second* kiss they had exchanged, meant nothing. Nothing at all.

When she pulled into her driveway she was crying. Because she knew in her heart—where it counted most—that the kiss had meant everything to her.


"Oh, sweetheart, don't cry," Erin's mother admonished gently as she pulled Erin against her for a farewell embrace.

Erin blinked back the sloppy tears that threatened to overwhelm her. "I'm going to miss you, Mom."

"Your father and I are going to miss you, too, honey."

Behind the boarding pass counter, a uniformed woman spoke into the microphone, announcing the last call for her parents' flight. Letting go of her mother proved harder than Erin had expected.

As she stepped back, Joshua stepped forward. "Bye, Grandma."

Erin's mother knelt beside Joshua and gave him yet another hug. "Oh, sugar, don't grow up too fast while we're gone."

Erin glanced at her father. He had his reading glasses on and was checking their plane tickets—for the fiftieth time. Tenderness welled within her. He was as excited as a young boy beginning his first day of preschool. The familiar creases lining his aging face tugged at her heart, and she knew she'd miss both him and her mother tremendously.

He raised his head from the tickets. "Well, pumpkin, looks like this is goodbye for awhile."

Erin stepped forward into her father's wide-stretched arms for a final hug. "Be careful, Daddy."

"You, too, pumpkin—and take good care of that grandson of ours."

As he stepped back, Erin could see the moisture filming his eyes. "You bet I'll take care of Joshua," she returned staunchly.

In a final flurry of farewell waves and loving admonitions, her parents were gone. The doors to the jet tram closed. Erin held Joshua's hand as the people around them drifted away. After the airline personnel at the boarding counter left, the gate area was empty—save for Erin and Joshua.

"When will they be back, Mommy?"

"Not for a while, honey." Erin turned from the closed doors. "Come on, it's time for us to be on our way."

"I'm sleeping at Jake's house tonight, 'member? And we're going to the *circus!*"

Erin smiled indulgently. How could she have forgotten? Josh had talked of nothing else all day long. The big night had arrived when Teresa was taking the boys to the circus.

Erin wished she could share in her son's excitement. Until now, she hadn't realized her parents' departure would prove so wrenching. Being alone tonight was the last thing she wanted. As Erin and Josh walked to their car, she tried to shake off the cloud of despair that hovered over her.

During the drive home, Joshua babbled enthusiastically about the circus he and Jake would be seeing at the Salt Palace. Erin marveled at how easily he could be deflected from his obvious distress at his grandma and grandpa flying off on a giant plane without him. A rueful smile tugged at the corners of her mouth. Of course, few events in life could compete with a circus.

Erin was thankful traffic was light. With all the road construction around the airport, she had to keep her mind on the new exit ramps that had been installed. She was feeling nostalgic enough to find even those necessary changes depressing. Couldn't anything ever stay the same?

When they reached Teresa's house, Joshua began

wrestling with his seat belt. "Relax, honey, we made it here in plenty of time."

And then Joshua was struggling with his small suitcase and pillow. Her assistance mostly took the form of staying out of his path as he charged up the sidewalk to Teresa's front door.

"Goodbye, Mommy."

Laughing, Teresa stepped aside as Jake came racing out to meet Joshua. Soon the boys were inside the house. "I've never seen them so excited. Jake's talked about nothing all day except the circus."

"Joshua, too," Erin responded. "Well, I guess I won't keep you. You need to be on your way."

"Are you going to be all right?"

At the concern in her friend's voice, Erin's head snapped up. "Of course, I'm going to be all right."

"I should have picked up a ticket for you, Erin. I know your parents left tonight. It's a tough time to be alone. Maybe—"

"Will you stop it? I'm fine. Actually, I'm looking forward to having an evening all to myself. I intend to take a long swim and work out all the kinks."

Teresa eyed Erin with friendly envy. "Lady, if you've got a single kink, I don't know where you've hidden it. You're in such terrific shape, it's disgusting."

Despite her gloomy mood, Erin laughed. "Gee, thanks a lot."

"I mean it," Teresa returned seriously. "And I'm not just saying it because I'm pregnant. Let me tell you, all up and down the street a lot of husbands are standing by their windows when you take your morning run."

"You should be a writer," Erin said. "You've got the most active imagination of anyone I know."

Teresa's booming laugh rolled loose. "See ya tomorrow afternoon, honey. Don't worry about Joshua, I'll take good care of him."

"Have fun," Erin called over her shoulder as she headed toward the car. Her spirits were lighter for the brief conversation with Teresa. Erin could almost believe that she was looking forward to a night alone.

Almost...

# Chapter Eight

It was inevitable, of course, that she would think of Linc and the kiss they'd shared in the conference room. Idly, Erin skimmed her fingertips across the pool's pleasantly heated water. The lights were on and a buoyant wake of fluorescent bubbles followed the gesture.

Deliberately Erin forced herself to think of something besides Linc. By now her parents had reached Los Angeles and were settled in their hotel room. Joshua was probably stuffing wads of cotton candy into his mouth and squealing at the high-flying, death-defying swoops of sequined aerial artists.

At least trapeze artists worked with nets, Erin mused grumpily as she pushed off and floated on her back across the pool—she'd already swam her hell-bent, throttle-out, leg-pumping laps.

In the night sky above her, wispy black clouds scuttled across the moon. The darkness imbued everything with a sense of unreality. Despite the pool's steamy warmth, she shivered.

Stubbornly, her thoughts returned to Linc Severance and how it felt to be kissed by him. She sighed. Surely high-flying somersaults were no more terrifying. She reached the edge of the pool and turned, kicking off for another leisurely float across the water.

She tried to summon the other bits and pieces of the day into focus. There was Joshua, so excited about the preschool and the circus that his grandparents' departure had paled in comparison. Erin wished she'd thought ahead and asked Teresa to buy her a ticket for the circus, too. Maybe a mouthful of cotton candy while watching dancing elephants would give her spirits a boost.

When she reached the shallow end of the pool, Erin reclined lazily against the submerged steps. The water lapped gently at her waist, and she stared unseeingly into the night. She had a lot to be thankful for. Absently she cupped a handful of water and let it stream through her fingertips.

It was a matter of being content with what she had, Erin supposed. There was no point in longing for something that would always elude her—something like Linc's love. The words sifted through her mind without warning. It was a foolish thought, after all. What would she do with Linc's love?

A traitorous tremor tickled her stomach. Erin closed her eyes. All right, so it had felt wonderful to be held in his arms and kissed within an inch of her life. She couldn't lie to herself about not wanting the kiss. She *had* wanted it—with every fiber of her being. Had he not reached out for her, she would have been horribly disappointed. The hunger and desperation she'd sensed in him hadn't been any greater than her own desperate hunger.

So what did it all mean? That she was simply a woman with needs, as had been so tactlessly pointed out to her almost a week ago by Paul? Erin grimaced. It both comforted and disturbed her that her attraction to Linc could be dismissed as a case of overactive hormones. On the one hand, if the attraction was just physical, then she could justify it by the fact that she was indeed human, with human desires. Not that she was particularly comfortable with that side of her nature—she certainly never remembered feeling such overpowering sexual desire for Merrill.

No, with Merrill it had been more like the good-natured burst of energy one would experience at a sporting event. There was nothing good-natured about her shattering response to Linc. It had been dark and primitive and faintly savage. Erin kicked her legs slowly through the shallow water. It took dauntingly little imagination to visualize herself and Linc sprawled across the conference table in a blaze of erupting passions.

Despite the cover of darkness and being alone, Erin blushed. Good grief, what was happening to her? She had never been the kind of woman to occupy herself by imagining torrid love scenes. Of course, Linc was the kind of man who invited such fantasies. Had he always been so unapologetically sexy?

She thought back through the years she had known him and realized that she'd always admired Linc's physical bearing. In fact—Erin brought herself up short, uncomfortable with the direction of her thoughts and unwilling to pursue them. She had been a married woman. Even if she and Merrill hadn't had a particularly fulfilling marriage, she had been faithful to her late husband in all ways—even in her thoughts.

Or had she?

The question struck at the heart of Erin's value system. She pushed it aside ruthlessly. Even though Merrill's lovemaking had never transported her to the heights Linc's impassioned embraces had taken her, she had loved her husband. And a woman who loved her husband didn't think about other men. Erin had been raised to believe that. The answers were all there. She knew it. Perhaps she wasn't brave enough to ask the right questions. One of which might be, had she refused to accept the dividend checks because she'd known, on a subconscious level, that her refusal would bring Linc charging back into her life?

He stood in the shadows. Watching. He couldn't seem to help himself. The pool's floodlights highlighted every sensuous curve of the woman who had moments before been streaking through the water as if pursued by unseen demons. Something primitive tightened in his chest and...elsewhere. She was every man's fantasy. It was impossible to deny his incredible want of her. And want he did. To stroke, to taste, to become one with her.

Earlier the splashing sounds she'd made as she'd swum had held him transfixed. Nothing had ever sounded so erotic. He'd trembled at the image of her slicing through the pool, her wet body suspended in a florescent vacuum that invited—no *demanded*—his trespass.

He watched her now as she relaxed on the pool

steps partially submerged. The sight of her water-slickened skin made his breath jam in his throat. The lazy movement of her legs tortured any sense of restraint. His body tightened, hardened. He reminded himself why he'd come tonight, even as he reminded himself that Erin had no way of knowing how much she tempted him. If there was anyone innocent in this affair, it was she. He would be wise to remember that.

Shakily Erin rose from the shallow water. The evening air brought a surge of goose bumps. She looked toward the darkened house. She wasn't ready to go inside and face her aloneness. Sinking into the warm water was easier. She closed her eyes, trying to find a measure of calm in her troubled thoughts.

There was no calm. The memory of Linc's image as his head lowered toward her ignited a slow-building heat that seemed to gather in her lower body. Beneath the slick fabric of her modest, one piece swim-suit, her breasts tightened. She jerked her eyes open. "Damn it, go away."

"But I just got here."

The quiet sound of a man's deep voice had Erin leaping up from the pool. Water sluiced haphazardly as she spun and pushed the hair from her eyes.

At the edge of the pool, with his suit coat slung casually over his shoulder, lounged Linc Severance. His pristine white shirt and perfectly knotted dark tie were at odds with his relaxed stance. He hunkered down, bringing himself eye level with her startled gaze.

For a reckless moment out of time, Erin simply stared. He seemed carved from the darkness itself, a compelling shadow of substance spawned by her very fantasy of him.

It hit her then in that highly charged moment.

Her feelings toward Linc Severance ran much deeper than physical desire. How else could she explain the wild burst of gladness that swept through her at his unexpected arrival? How else could she explain the wild hunger making her achingly aware that only a thin layer of fabric covered her nakedness? How else could she explain the shocking urge she experienced to wrap her fingers around his tie and pull his face toward hers?

"I thought I was alone," she answered, more than mildly astonished that her voice sounded normal—if one disregarded the quaver upon which the question ended.

"Swimming alone is dangerous, Erin."

*More dangerous than having you here?* "I can take care of myself."

"You've told me that before."

"Don't you think it's time you believed me?"

She would pick a fight with him, she decided. It was a matter of self-defense. If they were fighting, there was no danger of them succumbing to—

"But I can't believe you."

"And why is that?"

"Because if I do, then there's no reason for me to be here tonight."

She wished he hadn't caught her in the pool. Her lack of clothing was making it difficult to understand him, difficult to combat the rising level of attraction nipping at her composure.

"Why *are* you here?"

"I knew your parents were scheduled to leave tonight. I thought you might be feeling down."

Damn, he'd come on a mercy mission to patch up dear, brokenhearted Erin—again. Disappointment cut through her.

Her chin lifted and her eyes narrowed. "You missed your calling, Linc."

"Did I?"

She nodded. "You and my father seem cut from the same ministerial cloth. Both of you think too much about lost causes."

Linc leaned toward her and despite the night, despite the darkness, his eyes blazed with fury. *Good.*

"Don't call yourself a lost cause."

She shrugged. Linc's gaze dropped to her naked shoulders. The tension stretched tauter.

"Poor choice of words, I admit." Erin tried to adopt a blasé smile, but her lips refused to cooperate. Instead her glance fell to Linc's tie. The length of it dangled temptingly in front of her. How easy it would be to reach up and—

"It's time we cleared the air between us."

"Is it?"

His gaze held hers. "I don't want to hurt you."

"It hurt when you left last year without saying goodbye."

"I had to leave."

"So you said the first night you were back. I didn't understand it then, and I don't understand it now."

"You're shivering."

"What?"

He straightened and reached for the towel she'd

thrown across a redwood lounger. "Come out and dry off."

Erin eyed the thick, white towel he held above her. It looked very inviting, as did the strong hand gripping its outstretched edges. "You're being solicitous again."

He stared at her unblinkingly. "Is that such a crime?"

*It is when I'm on the receiving end.* She didn't speak the words aloud. They made no sense, after all. Obviously, Linc had stopped by tonight so he could tidy up their final parting. All she had to do was co-operate and she'd probably never see him again.

"What's going on in that beautiful head of yours?"

Startled, she tipped her head. "Do you think I'm beautiful?"

It was the kind of question that invited disaster. She knew it, knew she was opening a Pandora's box, but she couldn't help herself. Something wild, something strong and unconquerable was pushing her over the edge of the polite, circumspect behavior she'd followed for a lifetime.

"Come out of the water."

She sighed. There would be no pretty words from Linc, not tonight or any night. It was foolish for her to be disappointed. Slowly, she gathered her courage and walked up the steps into the folds of the waiting towel. Warmth engulfed her. Linc's warmth. His powerful arms followed the path of the towel as he wrapped it around her. She allowed herself another small sigh and leaned against him, looking toward the blackened silhouette of the Wasatch peaks.

A moment later he guided her toward the wide redwood lounger. "I'm not staying, Erin."

Was she supposed to be surprised? There was room enough for both of them on the lounger. They sat side by side, looking across the pool. The night, the man and her mood seemed a study of varying shades of darkness.

"This is going to be hard for me to say," he began, "but I've got a confession to make."

Her fingers tightened on the towel. What could Linc possibly have to confess to her? "Are you sure this is necessary?"

"Very."

The word was a low growl. Erin shivered.

Linc's arm came around her. "If you're cold, maybe we should have this conversation inside."

"I want to hear what you have to say now."

He was silent for a moment. "It's about the last night we were together."

"You mean when I fell asleep in your arms crying?" she asked softly, still embarrassed by her weakness with the man. The knowledge that she'd caved in when Merrill had died, and had depended so heavily upon Linc, still grated.

"Yeah, that's the night."

"I suppose I owe you an apology," she observed quietly.

"How do you figure that?"

"I fell apart on you— I'm sorry."

"Don't be sorry," Linc said, his voice gruff. "It meant a lot to me that I could be there for you. I needed to feel useful." He broke off reflectively. "I guess I needed to be needed. In this day and age, a man doesn't get that much opportunity to take care of a woman.''

"In this day and age, a woman likes to think she can take care of herself." But even as she spoke, Erin realized that the tables were shifting between herself and Linc. For once he was opening himself up to her, shedding his protective layers. She remembered once thinking of him as a dark horse. If that was true, he was coming closer to her than he ever had before.

"Yeah, the women's movement has almost made the need for men extinct." His tone was more than a bit disgruntled.

"I think it's more a matter of redefining our roles," Erin said softly. "If—if it wasn't because I was leaning too heavily on you, Linc, then why did you leave?"

It was a question whose time had come. She had to know what she'd done to drive him away.

"I stopped thinking of you as Merrill's widow and began thinking of you as...a woman."

Erin's breath lodged in her throat. She sat perfectly still, wondering if she'd heard Linc correctly.

"Well, aren't you going to say something?" he demanded with a ragged intake of breath.

"I—I don't know what to say," she admitted, wondering where this intimate conversation would take them.

"There you were, crying your eyes out because you'd lost your husband. I thought I was comforting you. You fell asleep in my arms..." Linc's recital became a monotone, as if he was locked in the past and reliving it. "I fell asleep, too. When I woke up, I was...I was caressing you."

An absolute silence fell. Erin had difficulty breathing. Linc's confession touched her deeply. She remembered all the times since his return that she'd been strongly attracted to him and her heart raced. "You were probably half asleep," she murmured for lack of anything better to say.

"That's no excuse. I took shameless advantage of you."

"You're being too hard on yourself."

"Before I left town again I thought you should know that it wasn't anything you did that drove me away."

*The implacable Linc Severance.* There were so many things that drew her to him—his unyielding code of ethics, his stubborn streak of integrity, his quietly nurturing nature. He was Merrill's opposite in a dozen different, a dozen significant ways.

Linc's admitted desire for her loosened a pulsing drumbeat deep within Erin. She surrendered to the ageless beat of that drum. Perhaps she didn't have the words to let Linc know he'd done nothing for her to forgive. But she could use another, simpler language. Slowly, stealthily, her fingers trailed from her lap to Linc's tie.

Beneath the light trespass of her strolling fingertips, he stiffened. "You're not making this easy for me, Erin."

The rasp of his voice told her of the struggle that was going on inside him. "On the contrary…"

She raised her face to him. His hands closed upon her arms and the towel fell away.

"Erin…"

"Linc…"

The gentle touching of their mouths was a slow dance of delight. His lips were warm, smooth and shut. Even so, having them rub lightly across her own lips scraped every one of her body's nerve endings to aching awareness.

He raised his head. Erin released his tie. She had ruined it. The tie. Wrinkled tracks left by her marauding fingers silently reproached her. She hoped desperately that she hadn't ruined something of far more consequence than his tie. The truth was she had no experience as a seductress. She was at the very edge of her expertise as a wanton, and was terrified her brazenness might repel Linc.

He stared long and hard at her. "You shouldn't have done that."

Erin drew herself up, seeking the inner steel she knew existed within her. "You've kissed me. Twice."

"A man only has so much control, Erin."

Erin blinked. "You think a woman has more?"

In the night stillness, his slow intake of breath was clearly audible. "What I think is that there's no way I can walk away from you tonight without making love to you."

Erin's gaze jackknifed to his.

With an abrupt movement, Linc drew back and rose from the lounger. He jerked his tie free and tossed it aside. Erin's heart hammered in her chest. She felt as if she'd awakened a slumbering dragon.

Linc's shirt became a blur of white as it joined his tie on the deck. Erin's stomach clenched. She didn't know what she'd expected—perhaps a slow build-up of tender kisses and loving caresses. The technical term was foreplay. She trembled. There was lot to be said for it.

Linc's hands were on his belt when he stopped and stared at her. "Now's the time to tell me to stop, Erin. In another minute there won't be anything but you and me, naked on that lounger. After that—"

"I want to make love with you, Linc." She raised her chin. "But if it's all the same to you, I'd like to slow things down a bit."

With dark eyes glittering, Linc stared at her. His hands were on his hips, showing to maximum advantage a wide swath of hair-roughened chest. From his clenched jaw and rigid stance, she deduced his displeasure at her announcement.

"You're asking a lot from me if you think the first time between us can be anything but hard and hungry."

"Are you trying to scare me?"

"Maybe I'm trying to scare myself, Erin. I didn't come here tonight for this."

She uncurled from the lounger and padded toward him, leaving the security of the towel behind. "It doesn't matter why you came, Linc. It only matters that you're here now."

"Dammit, Erin, I don't want to hurt you."

For the first time, she was forced to truly look at him. The moonlight wasn't kind. It revealed the icy rage that glinted from his dark eyes. Erin's impetuous passion died painfully, but it did die, killed by the look of raw anger in Linc's gaze. When she'd tried to seduce him, she'd overlooked one crucial piece of information. Even though he was attracted to her, Linc had no intention of acting upon that attraction.

It was clear he had no personal feelings toward her, and without them all he could offer was a swift, animal kind of mating. He had too much integrity to settle for that, and she, thankfully, had too much pride to ask for it.

But, oh, it hurt. Linc's rejection was too devastatingly similar to Merrill's when her late husband had told her that he didn't love her anymore, didn't want her anymore. Erin had experienced pain then, but that hurt was nothing compared to the chilling ache that squeezed her heart now.

Embarrassment joined the pain until all that was left was shame—shame and sorrow. She couldn't cry. She refused to cry. She refused to feel. She refused to—

"Don't look at me like that."

"Like what?" She tried for breezy and settled for coherent.

"Like I've broken your heart."

A protective, slow-burning fury began to grow with Erin. "Actually, my goose bumps are the only thing causing me any discomfort at the moment."

Her voice was stronger now. She was going to survive this devastating encounter after all.

"Erin—"

She tried another smile. It stuck. Barely. "Look, it's getting late, Linc. Since you've decided you don't want me after all, why don't you put your shirt back on?"

A low growl vibrated in his chest. "Knock it off, Erin. You know I want you."

"Right." She picked up the towel and wrapped it

around her. "As long as there aren't any feelings that go with the wanting."

"You just don't know how damned vulnerable you are right now, Erin. Only a heel would take advantage of you."

"You were perfectly willing a few minutes ago," she muttered, knotting the towel above her breasts.

"I'd be a liar if I said I didn't want to make love to you."

"I certainly wouldn't want you to perjure yourself."

"With your parents leaving tonight and Merrill gone barely a year, your feelings are bound to be mixed up."

"Don't patronize me, Linc Severance."

"I'm not patronizing you, dammit. Every time I get within ten feet of you, I want to drag you off to the closest bed. But that's just sex, Erin. You deserve more than that."

"Thanks for the clarification." She turned from him. "Now that you've delivered it, I suggest you leave."

He reached out to snag her arm as she tried to walk by him.

Big mistake.

Furiously, Erin rounded on him. "What is it you want from me?"

His lips thinned. "You— I want you."

She stared at him incredulously and jerked her arm free. "Well, I don't come without the feelings, Linc. Feelings like love and commitment and loyalty."

"That was for Merrill," Linc said, his voice hoarse. "Not me."

"Damn you." She shoved a hand against his chest. Hard. "What gives you the right to control what happens between us and then label it to suit your primitive code of honor?"

He grabbed her hand. "Push me again and I'll—"

"You'll what?" she challenged, so furious she could hardly choke the words past her rigid throat muscles.

"I'll finish what we've begun."

His words hung in the air like a menacing cloud. She tried to step back. His grip tightened. "The noble Linc Severance?" She laughed mockingly. "I hardly think that's likely."

"Push a man far enough, push him hard enough and you've got no guarantees."

"Is that what you think I need? Guarantees?"

"I think you need a husband and a rose-covered cottage. I'm not the man to give either of them to you, Erin."

"Wait until you're asked to."

He gave her a sharp tug and she staggered against him. "You asked, you taunted, you damn near seduced me."

A blistering blush fried her skin. "You've made your point. There's no need to rub it in."

"You're just too proud and too stubborn to admit that you were lonely for Merrill tonight and—"

"You think you know everything?" Goaded by demons she only half understood, Erin found the strength to rip free from Linc. "I've got news for you. It wasn't Merrill tonight, and it wasn't Merrill for almost two years before his death."

She pushed the wet hair from her face. "Merrill

didn't want me—not in his bed and not as his wife. The night he died he told me he wanted a divorce. I didn't make him feel enough like a man. I was too…too domestic, was the word I think he used. He wanted excitement in his life, and I couldn't give it to him.''

"Erin—''

''He didn't want to hear that I loved him, or thought I loved him.'' She rushed on, unable to stem the flow of words or tears. ''So don't think you owe me any explanations. I understand perfectly. If all you want from me is sex—short and simple, I can't give it to you. The feelings and emotions have to go with it, too. I'm sorry. I…''

Her tears caught up with her. Linc reached out to pull her into his arms. ''Honey, I didn't know.''

She raised her hands to ward him off. ''Oh, no, you don't. I don't want your sympathy. I don't want your understanding. I don't want your pity. I just want you to leave me alone. I never want to see you again.''

''I can't leave you like this.''

''You don't have a choice.''

For a long moment their gazes locked. ''I'm not going anywhere until you listen to what I have to say.''

She drew herself up. ''Save it. I'm not interested.''

He stared at her long and hard. Erin knew he was replaying their conversation in his mind. Trust Linc to try the analytical approach. Her anger was the only thing holding her together, but she didn't know how long she could hang onto it. She'd lost her pride. She refused to surrender anything else.

Slowly, he loosened the fingers that claimed her arm. "I know I've hurt you, Erin. But not as badly as I could if we'd let things get out of control. One day you'll see that this worked out for the best."

The *best?* She hoped she never experienced the worst. "I'm sure you're right."

His grip hadn't been hurtful, yet she found herself massaging her wrist. Still Linc stood immobile before her. What would it take to send him on his way?

"If I could change what happened tonight, I would," he offered tightly.

"Nothing happened," she reminded him stoically. "We kissed and then we backed off. It happens all the time. No big deal."

"Merrill was a bastard," Linc muttered, yanking his shirt from the deck and shoving his arms into the sleeves. "He didn't deserve you."

Linc's words shocked Erin. Always, she had believed her late husband and Linc were the best of friends.

Linc leaned forward, his face just inches from hers. "What you need to know is that I don't deserve you any more than he did."

Erin shrank away. "I'm tired, Linc. I can't take any more. *Please* go."

She hated that she had to beg. Somehow being reduced to that was the final humiliation. That and the hot tears licking at the back of her throat and behind her eyes.

His knuckles brushed her chin. "I'm going to miss you."

*Oh, damn him. He knew how to twist the knife, he did.* "I'm sure you'll recover. I intend to."

The words were puny darts tossed into the greater universe of his obvious indifference.

"I know."

"Well then, good night, Linc."

He muttered something crude and succinct under his breath, then turned from her. She felt the first tear break loose.

*Keep walking,* she silently commanded him as he faded into the night. She had no idea how long she stood alone after he'd finally gone.

A part of her couldn't believe he'd really been there, that she'd thrown herself at him and he'd rejected her. Stiffly, she moved toward the house. Why, oh, why had she behaved so shamelessly? She wasn't a seductress. Merrill had told her often enough that she didn't have a sexy bone in her body. What had made her try to seduce Linc Severance? She must have been out of her mind.

Or in love...

The thought stunned her, and Erin stopped with her hand braced against the door. No, she most certainly had not done anything as foolish as fall in love with Linc Severance. She'd much rather accept his explanation, that she was feeling alone and vulnerable tonight because of her parents' departure.

She straightened. Yes, that was the truth she would cling to.

# Chapter Nine

He'd screwed things up royally. Furious with himself and more than a little angry with Erin, Linc strode into his parents' house, slamming the door behind him. His reflection bounced to him from the floor-to-ceiling mirrors that lined the entryway. He came to a sudden halt.

His once neatly pressed shirt hung on him like a flag that had been dragged through enemy territory. His silk tie was trashed beyond repair, and he carried his suit coat in a wadded-up ball. Good Lord, he looked as if he'd fought his way back from purgatory. Who would have guessed Erin Clay packed such a wallop?

Linc continued through the house to the guest room. Last Monday when he'd sought out her company, he'd told himself he wanted only to make one last-ditch effort to convince her to change her mind about accepting the dividend checks. Tonight when he'd gone to her place, he'd told himself he was merely checking up on her. He understood now that he'd been deluding himself.

He went into the guest room he'd been using since his return to Salt Lake and hurled the rumpled ball of what had once been a twelve-hundred-dollar jacket into a corner of the room. His shirt and trousers soon followed.

What he'd been looking for tonight was a way for Erin and him to part as friends. When would he learn it wasn't in the cards for them to be just friends? Lovers, maybe—

The kiss they'd shared tonight had been pure fire. Lord, he'd wanted to wrap himself within that fire and make love to her more than he'd wanted to go on living.

When ice cold tendrils of water jetted from the shower head, Linc stepped inside and closed the glass door behind him. He let the high-powered stream of water batter him. It didn't help. His hands closed into fists. He remembered too clearly Erin's soft mouth opening for him.

Linc swore savagely. If Merrill were still alive, Linc would gladly kill Erin's husband himself for planting the doubt and hurt Linc had seen in her brown eyes tonight. But it was a hurt and doubt Linc wasn't entitled to heal. He shoved his face under the icy water. Who was he to think he could heal anyone?

A man twisting in hell was a poor choice for a rescuer. The water continued to pummel Linc. He turned off the faucet. He wasn't hard anymore. Wasn't that a victory of some kind? And he hadn't taken advantage of Erin.

He grabbed a towel and rubbed it ruthlessly over

his body. The minute Steve returned from his vacation, Linc intended to be on a plane bound for Los Angeles. He wouldn't see Erin again—not until enough time had passed for him to regain control over his rampaging lust. He figured that would be in almost twenty years—somewhere around the time Joshua was out of college.

Yeah, that's what Linc would do. Stay away from Erin completely. Before he did something they both regretted.

*Like believe for a minute that Erin could fall in love with him...*

Linc swore again, more basically. Like take Erin to bed and love her until they were both too exhausted to breathe. And he would make love to her, Linc thought grimly as he jerked the covers from his bed. There was no way on this good earth he could be alone with Erin Clay again without having her.

His thoughts scrambled for a burst of sanity. Erin had been vulnerable tonight. She'd been alone and lonely. A dangerous combination. When she'd virtually offered herself to him, she'd been thinking of Merrill.

No...

From her words about her late husband, he would have been the last man in her thoughts. Linc hadn't realized that Erin had been on her way to falling out of love with Merrill before his death. That discovery changed things, didn't it?

Hours later, when he finally drifted into a light sleep, the last image Linc saw was that of Erin rising from the pool. Soft and womanly and utterly irresistible. How had he found the strength to call a halt to their lovemaking? He knew he would never find that resolve again. Because she'd been off-limits to him for so long, Linc knew he was going to have to think through very carefully this next step with Erin.

With a sense of resignation, he accepted the fact that his attraction to her was growing, not diminishing. No matter how hard he struggled against Erin's pull, he felt himself being drawn to her. His noble intentions to walk away from her lay in ruins at his feet. Steve's words drifted back to him. Was his brother right? Was what was between himself and Erin too powerful to be denied?

Somewhere along the line, he was going to have to tell her the circumstances surrounding Merrill's death. Steve was right. The cover-up was going to have to end. There was no way there could be any kind of relationship between Linc and Erin until he'd told her the truth.

How would Erin feel about him then? How would she feel about the secret he'd kept from her? As a minister's daughter she'd been raised upon the Christian concept of forgiveness, hadn't she?

Linc stared thoughtfully into the darkness.

Erin sat at her sewing machine, concentrating on stitching an even side seam in the blue, furry material she'd bought for Joshua's Halloween costume. Two weeks had passed since the night she'd made a fool of herself with Linc Severance. She stopped sewing and pulled out the material to examine the seam. That's how she measured time these days. Before and after their encounter at the pool.

The seam would do. Erin held up the small costume. Joshua had insisted upon being a Smurf this Halloween. Since it was the first year she was taking him out to trick-or-treat through their neighborhood, she wanted him to have a special costume. He would look adorable, she decided.

She glanced around her sewing room and felt the emptiness of the house pressing in on her. Joshua had spent last night at Jake's again. The week before Jake had slept over at their place. Erin had never seen two little boys who were such good pals as Jake and Joshua. Maybe it was because they lived so close, or maybe it was because the boys were both the only children in their families. For whatever reason, no day seemed complete unless they spent time together.

Erin laid aside the costume and headed for the kitchen. It was an overcast day. The hint of an early snowfall iced the air. That's why she'd decided to sew a heavy costume for Joshua. The weather around Halloween was unpredictable in Salt Lake. The evening could be a balmy, fifty degree Fahrenheit, or the kids could be trudging through a foot of snow.

She decided a cup of herbal tea would hit the spot. Minutes later Erin wondered if the hot drink had been a good idea. Left alone with her thoughts and a mug of chamomile tea steaming between her hands, she found it appallingly easy to let Linc Severance take center stage.

He hadn't wanted her.

That was the final truth Erin had forced herself to accept. Somehow she'd been inadequate for him, just as she'd been inadequate for Merrill.

*Don't do this to yourself, Erin.*

In a couple of hours she would be picking up Josh.

If for no other reason than to keep up a brave front for her son, she had to fight the depression that seemed determined to steal over her.

It was no small thing for a woman to offer herself to a man and have him turn her down. Erin shoved aside the mug and began to pace. She must have been out of her mind to think a man like Linc Severance would desire her. Her skin burned with embarrassment.

She wanted to turn off her mind. She wanted to turn off her heart. What had she been thinking? What had made her think she could even make love with a man who wasn't her husband, especially when her religious roots went so deep she'd been unable to anticipate her wedding vows with Merrill?

But there had been something about that night, something about Linc that had almost convinced her she was falling in love with him. Surely she'd been deceiving herself about her feelings toward him, just as she'd deceived herself about her feelings toward Merrill. Hadn't she already proven she didn't have what it took to make a good wife?

*Wife?*

Erin stopped pacing and rocked back and forth on the balls of her feet. The last thing on this planet Linc wanted was a wife. Which worked out nicely, actually. Because that was the last thing Erin wanted to be. She'd learned her lesson. Some women could manage it. She couldn't—not with any degree of success.

Well, at least she wouldn't have to face Linc again. He'd obviously reached the same conclusions she had. He hadn't called or dropped by since the fiasco at the pool. Nor would he. She knew her old friend well enough to appreciate his stubbornness. No, there would be no reconciliation this time, no tender apologies, no risk of her repeating the gauche faux pas of telling a man bent on sex that she needed words of affection.

The phone rang and Erin reached for it automatically. "Hello?"

"Erin, turn on the radio."

The voice was Teresa's, a voice laced with panic. Fear clutched Erin's heart.

"What is it, Teresa?"

"That village in Mexico your parents went to, it was in the south, wasn't it?"

The fear became a leaden terror. "They went to Pulido, about as far south in Mexico as you can get."

"There was an announcement on the radio that there's been a major earthquake in that area."

"What?" Erin asked stupidly.

"Who can you call to find out if they're okay? The American embassy in Mexico City? Do you want me to call for you, Erin? Do you think I can reach them on a Saturday?"

The questions seemed endless. Erin tried to think, but couldn't. There had been an earthquake. Daddy had taken her mother to Mexico and there had been an earthquake. Her parents might already be dead, laying under—

"Erin, are you there?"

She stared at the phone. She couldn't panic. She couldn't fall apart. She had to function. She had to find out if her mother and father were alive.

The only problem was that she couldn't move, couldn't speak.

A thunderous pounding at the front door ricocheted through the house. Before she could react, Linc Severance charged through the kitchen doorway.

His face looked a hundred years older than it had the last time she'd seen him. His eyes were shadowed, his lips a stark line. Saying nothing, he crossed the room and took the receiver from her numb fingers.

"Who is this?" he asked simply, dragging Erin into his arms while he pressed the phone to his ear. There was a pause. "I've already gotten through to the embassy, Teresa. All the lines are down in the southern part of the country. I've got people working on getting through to Erin's parents."

There was another pause. Erin told herself to move from Linc's embrace. Yet she remained stationary, as if she'd been struck in bronze.

"You've got Joshua? Good, keep him with you. I'll bring Erin over in a few minutes."

He hung up the phone and turned to her. "Honey, it's going to be all right."

"It—it has to be."

Linc squeezed her. "I'm flying to Mexico. I'll check on them personally, make sure they're all right. I'm going to take you over to Teresa's now."

Erin allowed him to lead her into the hallway. His words finally sank in. "No."

He stopped. "You don't want to go to Teresa's? Do you want her and Joshua to come over here?"

Erin drew back. "You don't have to go to Mexico. They're my parents, not yours, Linc. We're not your concern. Go home. I can handle this myself."

From a detached corner of her mind, she watched an expression of cold fury fill Linc's dark eyes. "You're in no condition to—"

"I'm not going to argue with you. You're just going to have to accept the fact that I have no intention of falling apart like I did when Merrill died. This time I'm going to stand on my own two feet."

She skirted Linc and picked up the telephone. Calm now, she knew what had to be done. The first wave of shock was over. It was time she proved to herself and Linc that she could function in a crisis. As she punched out Teresa's number, Erin decided to go to the airport and buy a ticket for Mexico. Then when she was on the plane, she would figure out what to do next. Her parents needed her. She wouldn't disappoint them.

Teresa picked up the phone on the fifth ring. "This is Erin, Teresa. I'm going to ask you a really big favor."

"Anything," her friend answered. "You know that."

"Can Joshua stay with you for a few days? I'm going to fly to Pulido and check on my parents myself."

"But Linc just said—"

"Linc was mistaken."

"But to fly all the way to an earthquake area—"

"Will you keep Joshua?" Erin asked doggedly.

There was a pause, then a sigh. "You know I will, honey. I just think—"

"I'll stop by on the way to the airport and explain things to Joshua."

Erin hung up the phone, feeling much more in con-

trol of the situation. She moved past Linc to go upstairs and throw some things into a suitcase.

"I can't let you go," he said quietly.

"You don't have any choice," she answered without looking over her shoulder.

Once in her room, she pulled a suitcase from the
closet and began filling it haphazardly.

The sound of the small plane's propellers grated on
Erin's nerves, adding to her exhaustion. She remembered her son's words of a couple of weeks ago.
"When I die, Mommy, I want propellers." Looking
back, Joshua's wish seemed an eerie omen of impending disaster.

Erin curled away from Linc, who sat next to her,
reading an article from a magazine printed entirely in
Spanish. Briefly, she scanned his profile and puzzled
out the series of events that had culminated in his
becoming her traveling companion.

He had driven her to the airport, then watched as
she had been informed by one airline representative
after another that all flights into Mexico had been
temporarily cancelled. Her next efforts had been with
various private airlines and had also ended in failure.
Throughout the ordeal of burgeoning red tape, Linc
had made no attempt to interfere—until she had
sagged in defeat at an air freight counter six hours
after her arrival at the Salt Lake airport.

"I know someone who can help us."

She had looked at him, wanting to hurl angry words
of abuse. The words died in her throat. He looked as
weary as she felt. There was no way she could return
to the house and simply await word of her parents'

safety—she'd learned that such information could take days, maybe weeks, to obtain.

"I would appreciate you calling him."

No emotion had shown in Linc's flat gaze as he'd stepped to a phone and called a number jotted in a small, leather-bound book. Linc had asked a few terse questions of a man called Tiny, then hung up. Then Linc had dragged her to yet another ticket counter, this one a major airline. Less than thirty minutes later they had been on a flight bound for Los Angeles, where they'd made connections with Tiny and his sleek, twin-engine airplane.

Forty-eight hours later, she and Linc were nearing Trezone, Mexico, the nearest city with an airstrip to Pulido. Other than occasional catnaps, neither Erin nor Linc had slept. Both of them still wore the clothes they'd had on when they'd stood in her kitchen two days earlier.

Again Erin's gaze drifted to Linc. A heavy growth of stubble covered his jaw, adding an element of menace to his harshly chiseled features. In keeping with his unflappable aura of command, his suit was remarkably wrinkle free.

Erin tried not to resent him for his control or his unrumpled state. Because she failed, Erin shifted farther from him. Her own hopelessly crinkled tan slacks and pink blouse, replete with the smell of stale cigarette smoke, tea stains and dried perspiration, made her feel grubby and out of sorts.

Erin's eyelids drifted shut. An unexpected peace had claimed her once she and Linc were actually on their way to Mexico. Perhaps the prayers she'd silently uttered had something to do with her growing calm. The moment she had faced a life-threatening crisis, her upbringing had automatically kicked into gear. As the awful possibility of losing her parents had gripped her, a quiet peace had steadily prevailed over the terror, almost as if an unseen force was reassuring her that everything would be all right.

Erin sighed, giving in to the monumental tiredness within her. Maybe she would rest for a few minutes...

She shifted against the comfortable support that cradled her. A lovely dream held her in gentle sway. She knew it was a dream, because she was almost awake, yet she couldn't let go of the sweet vision that cocooned her.

Her face was tilted toward the sunlight. She was laughing. Her mother was pushing Joshua in a swing as her father stood close by watching. Higher and higher Joshua flew, until his small, outstretched feet touched the clouds themselves. A shadow fell across Erin. Comforting arms descended around her shoulders. She leaned back.

*"I was waiting for you,"* she said to the companion who stood behind her.

*"I've been here all along."*

*"I didn't see you."*

*"You weren't looking."*

*She twisted to see over her shoulder.*

Slowly Erin's eyelids opened. Linc held her. Their gazes locked. His was narrow, naked with longing. Erin was held in thrall. Her surroundings came slowly into focus. She was in a plane. She was nestled in Linc's arms, sitting practically on his lap. It seemed important that she disentangle herself, but her body had become so relaxed, she was unable to move.

"You fell asleep."

His voice was a seductive murmur. He made no effort to release her. She seemed to remember she was angry with him, but she couldn't recall the reason. Her fingers drifted to the bristles on his hard jaw.

"You need a shave."

His lips curved with a slow smile. "I guess I do."

"What happened, Linc?" she asked softly. "What happened to us? We used to be friends."

"I guess life happened." His smile twisted. "I'm here for you now, Erin."

But now wasn't nearly enough for her, she discovered. It hurt that it could be enough for Linc. "You make a nice pillow."

"Thank you," he answered with formal dignity.

"Linc…"

"Your mother and father are going to be all right, Erin," he assured her with a gentle squeeze of her shoulders. "We're going to find them safe."

She wanted to believe him, just as she wanted to believe the still, small voice within her that offered the same assurance. "It won't be long now, will it?"

"Tomorrow," he answered quietly. "We'll find them tomorrow."

She wanted to kiss him. She wanted to wind her arms around his neck and draw him to her. She'd learned her lessons well, however, and remained motionless in his embrace.

They found the first sign of the quake that had rocked southern Mexico in the city of Trezone. In places the airstrip had buckled to mounds of loosened cement. At dusk their pilot, Tiny, all six foot four, two hundred and sixty pounds of him, had brought his plane down in what he'd later declared was a "damned fine bit of flying" on a hundred yards of undamaged runway.

The city was without electricity or water. None of the phones were operational. There was no information about Pulido, which was a six-hour drive from Trezone—on a road noted by the locals for its difficulty to traverse.

When the plane had finished its bumpy landing, Erin had been surprised that the cargo doors had opened and relief supplies were hauled into a waiting truck. Shamed by her lack of thought in that regard, Erin rode silently in the borrowed truck. Once they arrived in town, the boxes of supplies were immediately thrust into waiting hands.

The rapid-fire Spanish being spoken around her and the sultry curtain of falling night made Erin aware of the unfamiliarity of her surroundings. She stayed close to Linc. When he took her arm to guide her toward a low stucco building, she followed him without question. It took a few moments for her to realize they had entered a tiny hotel lobby.

She looked at Linc blankly.

"There's no way we can drive to Pulido until morning. No one knows what condition the road is in. They're too concerned with taking care of their own needs. I got a room for you here tonight so you can sleep in a real bed. Tiny assures me this is the cleanest place in town."

Linc picked up her suitcase, and Erin reached out to put a restraining hand on his arm. "Wait a minute. Where will you be?"

"They only had one room." He shrugged. "I'll sack out in the plane."

Erin looked at the strange surroundings and shivered. "I don't want to be alone."

Very carefully, Linc loosened the grip of her fingers. "You'll be okay. Tiny says—"

"I don't give a damn what Tiny says. There's no way I'm going to stay here by myself."

"There's only one bed, Erin."

She took hold of his arm again and urged him forward. "We can share it."

"Just a minute—"

She interrupted him again. "Relax, you're virtue's safe with me, Linc. I have no intention of attacking you while you sleep and having my wicked way with you."

He said nothing, but he did continue accompanying her along the hall, obviously straining to read the room numbers in the dim light provided by the flashlight he'd carried from the plane. Finally he stopped and pushed open an unlocked door. A very small-looking double bed greeted them.

Briskly, Erin stepped forward. "Do we have our own bathroom? I'd love to shower."

Linc set down her suitcase and shined the beam of light toward the bed. "There's no water, Erin."

That's right, there had been an earthquake. She drew her fingers through her hair and stalked to the bed, the only part of the room of which she had a reasonable view.

"Then let's get some sleep. I want to leave first thing in the morning."

The only things she removed before she slipped

between the faded sheets were her shoes. The flashlight continued to shine while Linc remained standing in the center of the small room.

"Shut off the flashlight and come to bed," she ordered in a no-nonsense voice.

Immediately the room darkened. Erin heard him step to the other side of the bed.

"I can't sleep in my clothes," he announced. The slick rasp of clothing being removed followed.

She rolled to her side, away from him. "Fine."

She supposed she ought to be concerned with how much of his clothing he intended to remove. Just as she ought to be concerned about the not-so-distant small scurrying sounds she heard. But her eyelids weighed a pound apiece, and she could no longer hold them open over her burning eyes. All she had the energy to do was savor the sensation of being stretched out in a horizontal position.

When the mattress dipped significantly on the other side of the bed and gravity pulled her toward the middle, Erin halfheartedly struggled to hold onto her edge of the mattress.

"Linc?"

There was a long pause. "Yeah?"

"I'm letting you do it again."

"What?"

She frowned into the darkness. "Letting you do all the giving."

"You don't see me kicking up a fuss."

"You didn't want to sleep with me," she pointed out.

Another pause.

"I'm remembering how you felt in my arms that night at your pool."

"The memory is...unpleasant?" she inquired.

"No. It isn't unpleasant."

There were a dozen questions she wanted to ask. *Don't you feel anything toward me? Don't you want to explore what comes after friendship? Don't you want to hold me?*

"Thank you for getting me here," she said when she realized he had no intention of breaking the growing silence between them.

"Erin?"

"Yes?"

"I know there's things we need to talk about, but first we have to make sure your parents are okay."

He was right, of course. She rolled onto her side. For the first time since Merrill's death, Erin wasn't sleeping alone. It only felt that way.

Long before dawn, she awakened. She was pressed close to Linc's hot flesh. She forced herself to inch away from him, trying to do so without disturbing his sleep. She slipped from the bed and used the cover of darkness to remove her blouse, then bra. When that constrictive article of clothing was gone, she put the loose-fitting blouse back on, knowing she would sleep better. She bit her bottom lip, debating about whether to remove her slacks. How would Linc interpret such a gesture? Would he think she was trying to seduce him?

As grungy and tired as she felt, Erin discovered it didn't matter what Linc thought. The slacks joined her bra on the stand next to the bed. When she returned beneath the sheets she felt much freer. Sighing, she turned her back to Linc. Sleep came easier the second time around.

The caress was whisper soft, a slow, sensual stroking of her most sensitive flesh. Erin opened her eyes. She knew where she was. She knew whose hand lay beneath her blouse, fondling her breast. She squeezed her eyelids shut to better savor the wonderful sensation of being touched by a man's strong hand. Liquid heat gathered between her thighs. She lay absolutely still, not wanting Linc to know she had wakened. She supposed she should be outraged by the liberty he was taking. But his caress felt so good, she was unable to summon anger.

Her legs shifted restlessly against each other. Deliberately she turned slightly so Linc had fuller access. His fingers explored the rigid thrust of her hardened nipple. She choked back a moan, unable to suppress a tremorous sigh.

She needed to touch him, no longer caring if he knew she had awakened. She reached out to him. Her fingertips sank into a carpet of lush hair.

He groaned.

She lost herself more deeply to the sensual spell that held her in its enveloping folds. His body was a contrast of rigid muscle, silky hair and musky scents. It felt good to be held against his fiery heat.

His palm tightened perceptively upon her breast, and she shuddered with pleasure. To lay with her body tight against his, to feel his unmistakable arousal against her hip, to have the weight of his hand intimately stroking her breast left Erin no alternative but to seek the release for which her throbbing body burned.

"Linc…"

"Don't move."

His words were a guttural moan. Instantly, she froze, thinking that some terrible danger threatened. "What is it?" she whispered.

She tried to perceive what it was that menaced them. An armed intruder? A snake?

"It's you." He eased slowly away. "It's always you, everywhere I turn."

A dull morning light filled the room. With the light came reason. Memory. Erin brought her trembling hands to her face. "I'm sorry, I guess I was taking up more than my half of the bed."

The sound of an angry zipper rent the air. "You got that right."

Erin lowered her hands and sat up. The situation was embarrassing enough without Linc making a federal case of it. "Look, I said I was sorry."

His head snapped up, and he jammed his arms into his shirt. "What do you think I'm made of, steel? Do you know what it does to a man to get so hard that he—" Linc broke off with a curse. "Get dressed. We need to be on the road."

Erin tossed back the covers and leaped from the bed. There was nothing she could say in her defense except… "You started it."

Linc's dark eyes narrowed. "How do you figure that?"

She scooped up her bra and slacks and headed for

the bathroom. "I was asleep, Linc, minding my own business when I felt this hand—and it wasn't mine—caressing me." She straightened. "Here's a bit of news for you. I'm not made of steel, either."

# Chapter Ten

The vintage Jeep had its work cut out for it as it lugged in low gear up the rutted dirt road. Erin braced herself against the door to keep from being hurtled out. For the first time, the alienness of her surroundings fully penetrated Erin's fear and anger.

The thick, humid air that pressed against her was so different from Utah's dry mountain air. Lush vegetation grew in steamy heaps of unending green. She shaded her eyes against the rays of the rising sun and tried to take comfort from the fact that she saw no sign of earthquake damage in the area. The land was so primitive, so undeveloped, though, she supposed it would be difficult to tell.

There had been damage to Trezone. Several roofs had caved in. A few adobe buildings had crumbled, and in some places the road lay raised in buckling ripples. The Jeep took a particularly nasty dip, and Erin held onto the door for dear life. Linc ruthlessly ground the gears. The fact that he didn't swear, that he maintained his rigid, jaw-clenching silence didn't escape her.

It required superhuman force, but she tore her glance from his unyielding profile. He had no right to be angry with her. A woman couldn't be held responsible for what she did in her sleep. Besides, she, too, was paying the price of what had almost happened between them. Her body would never be the same, not after being aroused to such a feverish pitch and then dropped back to earth like a sky diver whose chute had failed to open.

The Jeep crested the hill they'd been climbing for the past thirty minutes. Below them lay a village bordered by a narrow river on one side and sprawling tropical vegetation on the other. Linc hit the brakes and reached for the tattered map he'd used to get them this far in their six-hour pilgrimage through the Mexican countryside.

"Pulido?" she asked, straining to see what effect the quake had had on the small town.

Linc folded up the map and shoved it into the space between them. "Yeah."

Erin concentrated even harder on trying to see down the boulder-strewn precipice. The Jeep bucked forward, then began a lurching descent that rattled her teeth and jarred her bones. Her grip tightened on the door. It wasn't the fear of falling out but the fear of what they would find when they reached the remote mountain village that paralyzed her.

*Oh, please, God, let my parents be all right....*

It took even longer to make the drive downward. Of course, it could have been her nerves that made it seem that way. At this point, Erin wasn't sure of anything.

When the Jeep came to a halt at the edge of the main road, the single road, leading through the pile of randomly built shacks, Linc shut off the engine. Through tears of relief, Erin saw that the quake hadn't struck the village. There was no way the crudely tossed together shacks could have survived even a minor tremor.

Poorly dressed men, women and children immediately surrounded the vehicle. Linc leaned over the driver's seat and lifted a heavy box filled with relief supplies. Seeing the gaunt villagers, Erin was again grateful for his foresight. She had only been thinking of her parents' welfare, but in the last hectic hours before Tiny had taken off from John Wayne Airport, Linc had been organizing relief efforts through local churches.

As he tossed the boxes into outstretched hands, Linc kept up a steady stream of Spanish. Finally, when the Jeep was unloaded, he turned to her, his expression satisfied. "Your folks are okay. They're working in a makeshift infirmary to patch up people from the outlying area who were hurt in a mud slide."

Erin brushed the tears from her eyes and sprang from the Jeep. "Where are they?"

"Just down the road." He came around the vehicle and took her arm. "I'll show you."

She supposed it was a natural gesture for Linc to touch her. She tried not to resent how good it felt to have physical contact of any kind with him. The rank smells of untreated sewage that occasionally reached her should have quelled any lingering stirrings of desire she harbored for Linc. Surely, there was nothing less romantic than raw sewage.

Erin smiled grimly. Love was an evil, vile, wretched trick to have played upon the human race. It made one weak in the heart, weak in the head and weak in the knees—not to mention messing up a person's olfactory system.

*Love?*

*Yes love, you fool. You've fallen in love with Linc Severance.*

Linc stopped and Erin, grappling with her sudden revelation, plowed into his back. He looked over his shoulder, his eyebrows raised. She ignored the implied question and kept going.

"Erin."

She whirled. *"What?"*

He pointed to a hut where a piece of dingy canvas was being used for a door. "Your parents are in there."

She swept past him and threw open the tarp. Her mother and father looked up from the child they were tending. Startled at the interruption, both their faces bore the same look of incredulity.

"Erin?" her mother asked, shaking her head as if seeing a mirage.

"Mother…" Erin stood numbly for a moment then crossed the small space separating them. Erin's arms came around her mother in a fierce hug. "Thank God, you're all right."

Erin's mother kissed her cheek. "Both your father and I are fine."

Erin went to her father and hugged him. "I was so afraid that you'd been hurt."

"The quake's epicenter was hundreds of miles from here," her father answered, also shaking his head as if doubting the fact Erin really was there. "Honey, we need to finish here."

Erin's mother had already returned her attention to the child sitting on a raised pallet. Erin realized the too-thin girl had a nasty cut on her forearm. Her father gently bathed the wound in a bowl of water. Beside the bowl sat a tall, square plastic container of bottled water.

Her mother spoke soothingly to the dark-eyed girl in Spanish, and Erin watched as the older woman carefully rubbed antiseptic over the girl's arm. Next to her mother's smooth hands, her father's larger hands worked with gauze. Above the child's sleek black hair, a look passed between her mother and father. The look was one of absolute love. In that moment, Erin realized how very deeply her mother and father loved each other.

"We're almost finished here, Erin," her mother said, looking up. She paused and shook her head. "I just can't believe you came all this way alone to check on us."

"I'm not alone. Linc came with me."

A look of relief swept her mother's features. "I should have known he would come with you."

Why should her mother have known that, Erin wondered. "He's waiting outside."

"Why don't you keep him company? We'll be done in a few minutes."

When Erin stepped from the shack, she walked a few feet from Linc and stared at what she now saw was a fast-moving mountain stream.

"Are you okay?" Linc asked as he came up behind her.

She turned, ready to tell him she was fine. The words froze in her throat. It hit her then. The memory of the look of love she'd seen on her mother's face. Erin knew she'd never looked at Merrill that way. Because her feelings for him had never been that profound, that soul-wrenching. She raked her fingers through her hair. It hurt so much to look at Linc and know that if he truly looked at her, he would see that kind of love mirrored on her own face—for him.

"Thank you for helping me get here, Linc."

"I always want to be there for you. That's what friends are for."

She studied him sadly. Was that all they were, friends? "Well, friend, you have my everlasting gratitude for your help."

He shrugged. "No problem."

Oh yes, there was a problem. She didn't want Linc in her heart or in her head. Twice, she had virtually offered herself to him, and he had turned her down on both occasions. Surely now was the time to start rebuilding the barriers that would keep the remaining vestiges of her pride intact. After everything that had happened between them, she'd have to be crazy to think she could unravel the mysteries of Linc Severance.

A shaft of sunlight highlighted his features as he stared at her from bloodshot eyes. A heavy growth of beard covered his hard jaw. With his white shirt at last looking rumpled, his tie gone and his suit coat abandoned in the Jeep, he reminded her of a disgruntled dragon.

Erin's heart tipped. She knew that as long as she lived she would remember this moment, this man. More vivid than any photograph on any mantel, her heart indelibly recorded his tousled appearance. And she knew that she truly loved him. Maybe... The thought shamed her. Maybe she had always loved him.

He ran a palm across his stubbled jaw. "Actually I enjoyed pulling everything together—even running wide of the law."

She stared at him in confusion. "Running wide of whose law?"

A glint sparkled in Linc's eyes. "Got your passport on you, Erin?"

She felt the color leave her face. "No."

"Me, neither."

"That means—"

He nodded. "We're illegal aliens."

She looked toward the Jeep. "But we brought aid and supplies."

"I don't think that matters to people who make careers of handling red tape. The point is we're going to have to enter the states by car through Tijuana. What with border concerns about drugs, it's too risky for Tiny to attempt to fly us back the way we came."

Erin looked at Linc in silence. All she could think was that the most straight-arrow man she'd known in her entire life—aside from her father—had blithely and without second thoughts broken international law for her.

"Erin, Linc, there you are."

At the sound of her father's voice, Erin turned. Lines of fatigue mapped his round face. He looked

older than she remembered and younger, too, somehow. Part of what was different about him, she realized, was that he wasn't wearing a suit. It seemed that
every time Erin had seen him since she'd left home,
he'd been dressed in a conservative suit. This afternoon he stood in jeans and a T-shirt. That was what
made him seem younger.

"Got another hug for your father, honey?" He held
open his arms expectantly.

"Oh, Daddy, of course I've got a hug for you."
She raised her face and kissed his cheek, wishing for
a moment that she was ten years old again and all she
needed was a father's embrace to make everything all
right.

That evening, Erin sat in front of an open fire with
Linc, her parents and the villagers. Her stomach was
full—not with the steamy beans and rice that had
been served but with some of the packaged food that
had been flown in. As Erin and Linc hadn't received
shots before entering the country, prudence dictated
they abstain from the mouth-watering native cuisine.

The day had been a long one and as she leaned
lazily against Linc, Erin didn't question why he'd
chosen to sit by her. It felt good to have his shoulder
available to cradle her. It felt natural, too.

Throughout the day, more mountain families had
trekked into Pulido seeking medical attention. Linc
and the villagers had pounded together a few more
shacks for the newcomers. All the medical supplies
and foodstuffs had been equitably distributed.

Erin thought of her life in Salt Lake, how comfortable and secure and self-indulgent it was. She ex-

perienced an onrush of pride in her parents for leaving
that kind of life to give something to the world. She
realized she didn't have to travel three thousand miles
to do the same thing, that there were people in her
own community who desperately needed the services
provided to them by…by charity. The word that had
caused her so much embarrassment in the past did not
come easily into her thoughts.

"Your parents are remarkable people, Erin."

Hearing Linc's words in her ear echoing her own
thoughts startled her. She stared into the crackling
fire. "More than I realized," she admitted.

"I envy you. As much as I love my folks, they
would never make the sacrifices your parents have."

"Through the years they've contributed heavily to
Dad's pet projects, though."

"Yeah, they've done that, and I know that's important. But I can't help feeling there's a greater sense
of reward when someone gets personally involved."

Erin thought of the part-time job she was to begin
next month. Those same hours could be used for vol-
unteer work at the elementary school or the hospital.
She was in the financial position to do that and still
provide for Joshua.

The thoughts were so contrary to the way she had
been thinking, Erin wondered if her parents' zeal was
somehow contagious. Her gaze went to them as they
sat close to each other. Why hadn't she ever recognized how deeply her mother loved her father? Erin
watched as he stood and pulled her mother to her feet.
They came to where Erin and Linc were sitting.

"Erin, honey, we're going to call it a night," her

mother said. "We've made up bedrolls for you and
Linc next to ours."

Because there had been an aftershock that afternoon, the villagers had chosen to sleep outside.
"Good night," Erin called after them.

Linc added his good nights, but he and Erin remained before the fire. More time passed. Erin wished
there was some way to stop its inexorable passage.
She had the feeling that this would be one of the last
nights she would spend with Linc before returning
home to Joshua and beginning the new life she'd
charted for herself—a life without Linc.

She sighed.

"Are you worrying about Joshua?" Linc asked.

"No, I know Teresa's taking good care of him. I'm
just missing him."

"He's a very lucky little boy."

"Why do you say that?"

"Because he's got you for a mother and your folks
for grandparents."

*But he doesn't have a father.* "I'm the lucky
one—to have him for a son."

"He's quite a character," Linc observed quietly.
"I'm going to miss him when I go back to Los Angeles."

*Don't go...* Erin couldn't say the words. From his
behavior toward her, Linc had made it very clear that
he didn't want to be involved with her. Oh, his sexual
attraction was obvious, but it was just as obvious he
found that attraction abhorrent. She pulled away from
him and wrapped her arms around herself, trying to
ignore the emptiness within.

"He'll probably miss you, too," Erin confined herself to admitting.

They lapsed into silence again. The fire burned down to glowing pieces of wood. Gradually Erin noticed that she and Linc were the only ones who hadn't drifted off to bed.

She got to her feet reluctantly. All great journeys began with a single step. She needed to start getting used to being without Linc. "I guess it's time for me to say good night."

Linc rose. "I'll walk with you."

"That's not necessary."

"We're going in the same direction, remember? I'm sleeping in the bedroll next to you."

*But not with me...* "I'm going to walk a bit."

Linc glanced around the rugged, moonlit terrain. "I don't think it's a good idea for you to go off alone. You might get lost."

Erin laughed softly, cocking her head toward the river. "Let's see, it's about thirty feet on a straight path, dead ahead to the riverbank. I think I can manage to keep my bearings."

His expression remained serious. "I'll walk with you."

"You're not invited." It was a silly point over which to quarrel, but she had to draw the line somewhere, and somewhere seemed to be in a mountain valley in southern Mexico.

He frowned. "You're being childish."

She raised her chin. "You're being domineering."

"You've got to be exhausted, Erin," he began, evidently deciding to use a new tack to change her mind.

"I'm not going to be able to fall asleep until I wash some of this dirt off me."

"Still—"

"Good night, Linc," she said, turning from him.

When he didn't accompany her down the path, Erin smiled. Assertiveness was just a matter of standing firm.

At the riverbank, she veered north. Actually she had more in mind than splashing cool water across herself. Her mother had mentioned there was a small lagoon, complete with a waterfall, just a few yards from the main access to the river. According to her mother, the women of the village bathed there each morning.

The path curved around a large stand of jungle foliage. Erin came to a stop. The moon provided enough light for her to see the small waterfall with perfect clarity. The sound of water falling from a distance of five feet and splashing into a darkened lagoon seemed the stuff of fantasy, not quite real. That was okay. There was nothing wrong with a little fantasy, especially when real life was often so grim.

She peeled off her blouse and decided to rinse it before she bathed. Since everything in Pulido was damp at all times anyway, it made little difference that the material wouldn't have time to dry. She was kneeling on the ground, wringing the excess water from her blouse, when she felt more than heard someone come up behind her.

She jerked around, shielding herself with the wet fabric. "Who is it?"

"Relax, Erin, it's just me. I got worried when I walked to the river and didn't see you there."

Knowing it was Linc standing in the shadows returned her heart rate to normal but in no way diminished her anger.

"You're a menace, Linc Severance. You're the one who needs a keeper."

"Sorry I startled you. No harm done."

"Other than scaring me half to death," she muttered, getting a better grip on the blouse she held pressed to her chest.

He leaned against a large, accommodating rock and folded his hands across his chest. "I'll stand guard while you wash off and then walk you back."

"Do you need a telegram to get the message? I don't want you here."

She made her announcement through gritted teeth. Getting caught half-dressed by Linc brought a vivid reminder of how it had felt to have their hot bodies lying intertwined in bed. She swallowed. Just as vivid was the memory of the night they'd come close to making love at her pool.

"I don't think Western Union delivers out here."

"Linc..." She sucked a calming breath into her lungs. The sweetly moist texture of the air did nothing to soothe her. "I'm going to spell this out for you. I intend to bathe naked in this pool of water. To enjoy doing that, I don't want you watching me. Ergo, I need to be alone. Now get the hell out of here."

"I thought you were going to cut out the swearing?" he drawled.

"Are you deliberately trying to make me angry?"

He straightened. "Now why would I do that?"

*Because you're the most contrary man I've ever met?* "I don't know." She stared across the short distance separating them, wishing she knew what thoughts he hid behind his shadowed expression. "If you want to play watchdog, walk down the path a few feet and give me some privacy."

"I could always join you…"

A palpable sexual tension suddenly filled the small clearing. "Yes. Yes, you could, Linc."

She would offer no further encouragement. Too often she'd opened herself to him, admitting her physical and emotional needs for him. If the distance between them tonight was to be closed, he would have to be the one to close it.

"I guess you know I want to."

"What's stopping you?"

She held her breath, her fingers tightening on the bunched-up blouse she pressed against her. The waterfall continued to cascade to the lagoon behind her. She could hear the splashing. Other than that, it was as if nothing on the planet moved. There was only her and Linc. Standing together. On the brink.

"Merrill."

"Wh-what does he have to do with this, with what's happening between us?"

Linc groaned. "Only everything."

"I—I don't understand."

"I remember how much you loved him. I can't help thinking when we're together that I'm standing in for him."

Erin's thoughts whirled to the common past she and Linc shared. "*Did* I love him? Lately, I've begun thinking that it was more a matter of me being swept off my feet. Oh, at the time I certainly thought I loved him, but now that I've grown up a bit, I'm afraid I let Merrill's sophistication and wealth blind me to our differences.''

Linc pushed off the rock and moved toward her. "Differences?"

She shrugged. "I've already told you things were pretty shaky between us. Merrill wanted a divorce."

Linc's arms came around her. "He was a fool."

All the emotion, all the pain she'd tried to choke back rose up inside her. "I feel so guilty, Linc."

"About what?" he growled in her ear.

"About not loving Merrill the way he needed to be loved. I let him down. I failed him. If—if we hadn't argued the night he died, maybe he wouldn't have been drinking and wrecked the car."

Linc shook her. "Listen to me, Erin. You were a good wife to Merrill. I was there. I remember. You may have been out of love with him when he died, but I'll never forget how you looked on your wedding day." He broke off for a moment. "As long as I live, I'll always remember you coming down the aisle in your wedding gown. You were radiant...glowing."

Linc's words offered needed solace. Erin wept softly against his chest, feeling as if a great burden had been lifted from her shoulders. She'd needed desperately to hear what Linc was telling her. His words absolved her of guilt. She had loved Merrill as deeply as her girlish heart had permitted, but those feelings had simply never matured into the all-encompassing love she'd seen earlier today on her mother's face. The kind of profound feeling she had for Linc.

Slowly, Linc eased away from her. He tilted her face toward him. The moonlight revealed his tortured expression.

"There's no reason on this earth for you to feel guilty about anything. Merrill was responsible for his actions the night of his death—not you."

"But it was because of me that he'd been drinking and driving. That's one responsibility I'll have to accept and live with the rest of my life."

"He wasn't alone."

Erin stared at Linc in astonishment. "Of course he was. He—"

"Someone else was with him that night."

"But—but that can't be true. The police report would have mentioned someone else being in the car."

"She left the scene of the accident."

"*She*…" Erin's voice shook. It was as if Linc was suddenly telling her the earth was flat. "I don't understand."

"Merrill was with another woman the night he died."

"Why didn't she come forward and—"

"Her family wanted to protect her. She called them from Merrill's car phone. They arrived before the police—or the ambulance."

Sickness twisted her stomach. New tears burned her eyes. "How could she have left Merrill alone and not waited for help to arrive? And how did you find this out?"

"After the accident, I took care of disposing of Merrill's car. I found the woman's purse, put two and two together and confronted her."

"But you should have gone to the police. What she did was wrong. She—"

"She was seventeen, Erin. Something like that

could have ruined her life and it wouldn't have brought Merrill back. And—'' Linc shuddered ''—it would have needlessly hurt you.''

Erin remained immobile in Linc's embrace. Her eyes were dry now. A growing coldness filled her. ''All this time, for more than a year, you've kept this from me.''

''I never planned on telling you what had happened, but I didn't know you were carrying guilt around for Merrill's death. You needed to hear the truth.''

''So how does it feel to play God?'' she asked brokenly, wrenching herself from Linc's hold.

''Like hell,'' he answered softly.

''How weak and pathetic you must have thought me to be,'' she mused darkly. ''All those times you comforted me after Merrill's death... It was only pity motivating you, not friendship.''

''Erin—''

''And you knew about Merrill's women.''

''Merrill never kept them a secret from me.''

''Well, he kept them a secret from me!'' Uncaring of any modesty, Erin shook out the crumpled blouse she'd been clutching and put it on. ''It was only in the months after his death, after you'd gone back to Los Angeles, that I found his journal.'' She laughed sarcastically. ''Such an elegant name for a book listing the names and dates of his conquests.''

''I wanted to keep you from being hurt, Erin.''

She shoved her hair from her face. ''I can see that. You were just being...protective.''

''You needed protecting.''

She flinched. ''Well, you did your good deed, Linc.

I'm going to stop blaming myself for Merrill's death.''

Linc looked into the distance. ''I knew you would be furious when I finally told you the truth.''

''You're mistaken, I'm not furious. After all, it's old news, isn't it? Please leave me alone for a few minutes so I can wash off the dirt and go to bed.''

''I'll wait for you down the path.''

*Her ever-faithful watchdog.* ''I won't be long.''

## Chapter Eleven

In the predawn hours, Erin opened her eyes. It took her a moment to remember where she was, and why. The earthquake, the frantic flight with its seemingly endless series of refueling stops before she'd been able to see for herself that her parents were all right—Pulido, Mexico.

And Linc...

She stared at the overcast sky. Despite her tiredness, she had lain awake half the night thinking of the things he'd told her by the waterfall.

And waterfalls were supposed to be such romantic places...

She knew Linc well enough to know his words had been meant to assuage her feelings of responsibility for contributing to Merrill's death. And in some strange way, she realized his explanation had freed her from the burden of guilt she'd carried. But Linc had seen her as an object of pity, not love. That was the bottom line.

Maybe it was a matter of habit. Maybe Linc was so used to thinking of her as a friend that he couldn't see her as a woman. The memory of his body pressed hard against her own demolished that theory. She knew Linc was very much aware she was a woman.

Her thoughts came full circle. Just because a man wanted a woman didn't mean he loved her. She sat up, hugging her knees to her chest. Tiny was supposed to fly her and Linc north today. The trip was going to take at least two days, with a night spent in Mexico City on the way. Maybe during that time she and Linc could begin again. If they could make a fresh start...

Erin got to her feet and groaned. Sleeping on the hard ground had stiffened every joint in her body. She threaded her way quietly through the occupied bed-rolls. Even though it was early morning, it was already warm. A light rain had fallen sometime during the night, adding to the general mugginess.

She glanced at the sky and wondered if they got very many sunny days in Pulido. Despite the gloom, she was feeling fairly optimistic as she walked to the Jeep to retrieve her suitcase. She planned to use the next couple of days to unlock Linc Severance's darkest secrets. Maybe when she discovered why he held himself in check around her, she would be able to show him that they could be more than friends. Much more. Maybe it was time he learned to open up to her, to share his feelings and his thoughts. Maybe he was as tired of being alone as she was.

When Erin reached the Jeep, the hood was raised. Two giant fists slammed it down, and she jumped back, surprised as the imposing mountain of Tiny's sweat-stained brown fatigues appeared in front of her.

"Tiny, my goodness, you startled me." She put her hand to her heart. "I thought you were still in Trezone with the plane."

"I didn't mean to scare you." He grinned apologetically. "I was just checking out the outfit. Are you ready to head back?"

Erin pushed at her hair and nodded. "I need to say goodbye to my parents first. Linc is still asleep."

Tiny shook his massive head. "No, he ain't. He drove into Trezone late last night."

"L-last night?"

"Yeah, it must have been a bugger driving there in the dark and the rain."

"I don't understand. You're supposed to fly us back to the United States. Why on earth did Linc go off by himself?"

"Don't worry. Linc sent me to get you. I'm still flying you to Tijuana. He's arranging for a car to pick you up at the airport and drive you through the check station."

"B-but how's Linc getting back?"

"Don't worry about him. He can take care of himself." With a meaty paw, Tiny wiped the sweat from his brow. "And don't worry about me getting you there safely. Linc and I go way back. He knows I'll take care of you."

Disbelievingly, Erin met Tiny's amiable gaze. She couldn't accept the fact that Linc would simply leave, that he would abandon her in this godforsaken place.

*You better start accepting it...*

"There must be some mistake, Tiny." There had

to be some kind of mistake. "Did he say there was an emergency of some kind?"

"He didn't say anything about an emergency to me, ma'am, just that he would make his own arrangements to get back to the States. Now if you wouldn't mind saying goodbye to your folks, I'd like to get on our way."

Stricken, Erin retraced her steps to the clearing. Her parents were up and speaking softly to each other. Her father saw her first. "'Morning, honey, how did you sleep last night?"

"Soggily," she answered. She took in her father's rumpled jeans and shirt and, despite her breaking heart, discovered it was possible to smile. "If any of your flock could see you now, Reverend Conroy—and you passed the plate—they'd probably be most generous."

Good-naturedly, he glanced at himself. "Look like a derelict, do I?"

She stepped forward and hugged him tightly. "Oh, Daddy, you look as if you're having the time of your life here."

Her father gathered her mother to him so that he had his arms around both women. "With your mother here to share this with me, there's nowhere else I'd rather be, sugar."

Bitter tears scalded the backs of Erin's eyes. She refused to let them fall. She wouldn't let thoughts of Linc's unexplained departure spoil this special moment with her parents. It would be a long time before she saw them again.

"Uh, Mrs. Clay?" The voice was Tiny's.

Erin kissed her father and her mother quickly, then turned. "I'm ready."

As they started the steep climb to leave the high mountain valley, Erin again found herself clinging to the Jeep for dear life. She glanced over her shoulder more than once at the steadily shrinking town. Then, when they crested the summit, Erin looked only ahead. She'd learned there was little point in looking back.

As for Linc Severance, he'd done the one thing for which she could never forgive him. He'd abandoned her. Again.

From now on, whatever turns her life took, she would experience them without Linc. As far as she was concerned, Linc was as dead to her as Merrill was.

"So, little brother, it's been over a month since you got back from Mexico. Are you ready to tell me what happened there?"

Linc scowled across his desk to Steve's damnably cheerful expression. "None of your business."

"At least tell me why you're still in Salt Lake. I figured when I got back from my vacation, you would hightail it to L.A."

"You figured wrong."

Steve scratched his jaw. "Mexico changed you."

Linc slammed several sets of architectural plans onto the table. "Don't you have some place you need to be?"

"Since Emily and I broke up, I've become a home-body."

Linc slumped in his chair. "I'm sorry about that. You and she seemed so right for each other."

Steve stared at his hands, then looked up. "I thought so, too."

"Do you want to talk about it?"

Steve's expression remained inscrutable. "You mean you want to hear about my troubles?"

Linc felt a stab of guilt that he'd been locked so tightly in his own unhappiness he'd ignored Steve's situation. "What are brothers for?"

"To kick each other in the butt when they drift off course?"

Linc laughed. "You going to bend over?"

Steve shook his head. "I was thinking of you, little brother."

Linc's amusement faded. "We were discussing your love life."

"At least I've got one."

"Had one."

Something dangerous glinted in Steve's eyes. "I'm hurting, I'll admit it. But you can bet I intend to get back in the saddle."

"Good for you."

"If it's good advice for me," Steve continued, "then it should be good for you."

"Meaning?" Linc asked suspiciously, not trusting his brother's cagey expression. Because Steve was the older brother, he had the mistaken notion he could manage Linc.

"Meaning, why don't you and I find us some women and do some partying?"

"I'm not in the mood to party," Linc answered

dourly. He pointed to the designs on his desk. "There's work to be done."

"So when was the last time you got lucky?" Steve asked, his tone conversational.

Linc's jaw tightened. "Let it go."

"I'm thinking in Mexico, maybe you and Erin—"

Linc was around the desk like a bullet. "What the hell are you trying to do, make me punch your lights out?"

Steve looked up from the chair in which he was still comfortably settled. "No, that wasn't what I had in mind. Of course, I'm not really sure you could do it."

"Dammit, Steve, don't play games with me. Just come right out and say what you have to say—but leave Erin's name out of it."

Steve stared him, not smiling now. "But I can't do that. She's at the heart of why you're so damned miserable."

"That's my business," Linc snapped. "And I'm not miserable. I've just been preoccupied."

"Go to her, Linc."

Linc closed his eyes. "I don't have the right."

"You love her, doesn't that give you the right?"

Linc opened his mouth to deny the accusation, then clamped his teeth. He wouldn't lie about that. He didn't think he could, not to Steve and not to himself, not anymore.

"Just drop it."

Steve got to his feet. "You love her, Linc. You have for years."

Linc grimaced. "I guess that's the point. I loved

her when she was married to Merrill, wanted her, too.''

The words left his chest in a painful rip. He'd held them so close to his heart through the years, that he felt as if a part of him lay rawly exposed.

"And probably felt guilty as hell about it," Steve mused aloud.

"She was married to my best friend."

"She was married to a selfish bastard who never had an inkling as to what kind of woman he'd lucked out in marrying. He threw Erin's love in her face by cheating on her. What kind of loyalty did you owe him then or now?''

Linc realized suddenly that he, too, had rejected Erin. Maybe for a more noble reason, but he'd rejected her just the same. He raked his hands through his hair. "Don't you think I've asked myself that a hundred times, a thousand times?''

"Well, ask yourself this, little brother. If you don't go after Erin, who do you think you're going to spend the rest of your life with?''

"The world's full of women, Steve."

His brother's features hardened. "Yeah, millions of them. But how many of them will have Erin's face or Erin's laughter? How many of them will have Erin's zest for living? How many of them will tempt you into a lifetime of lovemaking? How many of them have sawed-off little runts named Joshua who will call you Daddy?''

Linc swallowed the hard lump that had lodged in his throat. "None."

"Then forget the damned guilt you've heaped on yourself for being human. Go after what you want before it's too late. And remember this, it doesn't matter *when* you fell in love with Erin. It only matters that you did.''

Automatically, Linc's hand reached for the door. He stared at it in surprise, then looked at Steve. ''What you've told me about Erin goes for Emily, too. I know you love her.''

''But for some reason the lady's stopped loving me.''

''Maybe if you—''

''We'll save my love life for another time.''

Linc stared into his older brother's solemn eyes. ''Call Emily.''

Steve's gaze became thoughtful. ''I just might do that.''

The doorbell rang again. Erin watched Joshua pick up the large, orange pail of Halloween goodies before opening the door.

''Trick or treat!'' chorused a group of miniature goblins and ghosts.

Self-importantly, Joshua dropped a miniature candy bar into each out-thrust sack. Before Joshua had time to close the door, another group of children came rushing up the steps. He repeated the ritual, grinning from ear to ear.

As Erin watched him in his furry blue costume, she couldn't help smiling. This was the first Halloween that he was old enough to really join in the fun. She and Joshua had gone out earlier in the evening and knocked on the doors of their friends. Joshua's eyes had filled with gleeful satisfaction as his little sack of goodies had grown heavier with each house they visited.

Her son stared deeply into the orange bucket she'd placed beside the front door. "Are we going to have enough, Mommy?"

"There's more candy in the kitchen."

"If nobody else comes, can I have it?"

Erin smiled. "At the rate of one candy bar a week."

Josh thought that over and recognized a good deal when he heard it. "Can I put them in my pail?"

"Sure." Erin rose from the sofa. "And I'll keep your pail on the refrigerator."

Her son's forehead furled. There wasn't a doubt in her mind that he was contemplating the best way to climb to the top of the refrigerator. "On second thought, I'd better put it somewhere else."

"Where?" Joshua demanded.

"It will be my little secret," she answered lightly, as she scooped up his fallen Smurf cap and headed to the kitchen. "I'm going to wash the dishes. Don't open the door for anyone except monsters, okay?"

The bell rang again, and she watched her son dutifully look through the tall window that framed the door before opening it.

"Trick or treat!"

Inevitably, Erin's smile faded when she stepped into the kitchen and began clearing the table. These days it wasn't often that she smiled when she was alone. She was learning that getting over a broken heart was hard work. No wonder there were so many sad songs written about it.

*What if I had met Linc first, before Merrill?*

In the past few weeks it was a question she'd asked herself many times. Tonight was no exception in that she still had no answer. She shook herself mentally. She was doing it again, thinking about Linc. In frustration, she scrubbed her eyes with the back of her hand.

No more. She couldn't go on doing this to herself. It was time to admit once and for all that the attraction that had sizzled between them hadn't been any more than…than overactive hormones. In her head she understood that. Now, if only she could get her heart to reach that same acceptance.

*It's over. No more Linc. Can you understand that, heart?*

Her heart remained stubbornly hurt, as if it had been irreparably broken. She turned on the dishwasher, remembering the afternoon Linc had fixed it for her. Too bad she couldn't fish a wrench from the tool drawer and make a few adjustments to her heart.

Linc shut off the idling car engine. Every porch light in the neighborhood was lit. Here and there, groups of costumed children walked with their parents. Halloween… It hardly seemed an auspicious night to try to get his life back on track. He opened the car door and stepped out. The thought of seeing Erin again made his heart beat faster. It had been more than a month. His own fault, he admitted.

He remembered the night he had shown up at her door with the goal of getting Erin out of his life. What a fool he'd been for not realizing his earthly happiness depended upon having Erin *in* his life. Without her, his world had no meaning. What he hadn't understood

was that he was in love with her. For too long his
passion for her had overshadowed his softer, gentler
feelings.

That night at the waterfall in Pulido when he'd seen
how wrong he'd been to keep the circumstances of
Merrill's death a secret from her, Linc had thought
Erin would never be able to forgive him. And there
had been other demons for him to conquer.

Linc squared his shoulders and crossed the street.
No doubt she was furious with him. She had the right.
He'd walked out on her. He knew Erin well enough
to know that was something to which she wouldn't
take kindly. Possessive woman. For the first time in
weeks, he felt his spirits lift. He was a possessive
man. The way he figured it, that made them a perfect
match.

Linc stood to the side of a giant, leering jack-o'-
lantern that bore an uncanny resemblance to Horatio
the pumpkin, former resident of Erin's vegetable garden. Uneasy about Erin's reception tonight, Linc
pressed the doorbell. Would she even listen to him?
Or would she toss him out on his ear? Linc stiffened.
She'd listen. He'd see to it.

He glanced down the street. It was late enough in
the evening that only a few kids were still out. A blur
of movement through the window caught his eye, and
Linc looked down. Peering at him from the other side
of the narrow window stood a three-foot-tall blue...
something.

Curiously, Linc squatted to be at eye level with
what he deduced was a diapered blue rabbit—minus
the ears. Kids were wearing strange costumes these
days. Through the glass, Joshua continued to stare at

him as if debating whether or not to open the door. As he continued to gaze at the solemn boy through the glass, Linc felt the strangest sensation in his chest.

Pain. Pleasure. Anticipation. And a protective love that tied his stomach into knots. There seemed something symbolic about the glass separating them. That was how Linc had lived the last few years of his life, separated from those he loved, separated from the joy and the happiness, separated by an invisible barrier of guilt.

He prayed to God he had smashed through that guilt, but there was no way to break through the present barrier that stood between him and his future. The door had to be opened from the inside.

Down the street he heard someone call out, "Trick or treat!"

Linc felt more than a little foolish but he shouted the self-same words through the glass to Joshua. Immediately Erin's front door opened.

Trick or treat... It was a hell of a statement about his life and the times in which he lived that that should be the password to his future happiness.

"Hello, Joshua."

The boy held out an orange bucket. "Want some candy?"

It was the strangest thing, but Linc felt the back of his eyes burn. "What kind you got?"

Joshua named several familiar bars. "I'll take one of those," Linc said, pointing.

"That's my favorite," the boy confided.

Linc committed the fact to memory. "Mine, too."

They stared at each other for a few seconds. "My mommy's in the kitchen."

Linc's head jerked in that direction. "Yeah?"

"Uh-huh."

Linc felt as if he needed to say something to Joshua. Actually, he wanted to hug the boy, to ruffle his hair, maybe plant a kiss on his cheek. Embarrassed by the unfamiliar direction of his thoughts, Linc crammed his hands into his pockets. "So, what are you?"

"A Smurf."

"Any particular one?"

The boy straightened. "Hefty."

Linc grinned and started to compliment him on his choice when a bloodcurdling scream—Erin's scream—ripped through the house.

Linc bolted toward the kitchen. He came through the swinging door at a hundred miles an hour and skidded to a halt.

Erin was standing ankle-deep in water that was shooting out from beneath the dishwasher. Her wide brown eyes met his in obvious amazement at his unexpected appearance.

Linc moved to the sink and opened the cupboard door beneath it, reaching for the shut-off value. Three quick turns and water no longer gushed from the dishwasher. "I take it Mr. Lucco is still on his honeymoon?"

Erin pushed the hair from her eyes, feeling swamped by much more than sudsy dishwater. Water, it seemed, was to be her downfall with Linc—first the night at her pool, then at the waterfall in Pulido and now in her own kitchen.

"Linc Severance to the rescue," she muttered.

"Wow!" Joshua stood in the doorway, staring in

astonished delight at the inch-deep lake that had
formed on the kitchen floor.

"Stay put, honey," Erin commanded. "I need to
mop this up."

The doorbell chimed. "I'll give 'em the candy."

Joshua dashed off and the door swung closed behind him.

Erin had no recourse but to face Linc alone. "Why
are you here?"

His dark eyes glittered. "I couldn't stay away."

She slogged through the water to the tall cabinet
where she kept the mop, steeling her heart against
him. Loving Linc didn't mean that she could overlook
his casual tendency to disappear from her life whenever the emotions got too serious, too intense for him
to deal with.

"So how was your return trip from Pulido? Have
any trouble crossing into the United States?" she
asked.

Linc's fingers closed around the mop handle. "I'll
do it."

A brief tug of war ensued. Erin lost and wasn't the
least bit happy about it. "This is my house, Linc."

He nodded absently and applied the mop to the
floor. The minute the sponge came into contact with
the water, it was saturated. Linc held the mop over
the sink and flipped the spring to squeeze out the
excess water. "This is going to take awhile."

"I'll get some towels."

As she pulled old towels from the linen closet, Erin
reminded herself that Linc Severance was merely
passing through, as was his established pattern. The

fact that he happened to be in town and had stopped by shouldn't cause her heart to beat erratically.

For her emotional well-being, she *couldn't* let his presence mean anything. There came a time when a person had to get on with the rest of his life.

*Now, Erin,* she told herself. *Now is the time to be strong—for yourself, for Joshua.* As much as she loved Linc, Erin suspected he would never be able to forget that she had once been married to his best friend. Since it was impossible to change the past, she was going to have to accept the future, a future without Linc. The decision hurt, but not as much as it would hurt to open herself up to him and have him walk out on her again.

It's over, she kept repeating to herself as she returned to the kitchen. It's over. There was the familiar hot pressure of tears building behind her eyes, but she scarcely paid the tears any heed. Broken hearts hurt. She already knew that firsthand. But tomorrow *would* come and the pain would eventually recede. It was that thought that gave her the grit to step into her kitchen and act as if Linc's presence there was a commonplace occurrence.

It took more than an hour to set the kitchen to rights. After that, Erin bathed Josh and tucked him into bed. It was with a definite sense of déjà vu that she stared at her sleeping son. Almost two months ago she had stood just so, knowing that Linc waited for her downstairs in her living room, spoiling for a fight she'd wanted to avoid. She should have trusted her instincts and stayed away from him altogether.

She turned from Joshua and headed for the stairs. They wouldn't be arguing about dividend checks.

That dispute already had been resolved. So why was Linc back—just to aggravate her? To explain why he'd skipped out on her in Pulido? To say goodbye forever?

She found him stretched out on her couch, barefoot, his pants rolled up to his muscular, hairy calves. Again his habit of making himself at home in her house piqued her. "Thanks for your help, Linc. I guess you'll be on your way now."

Her hint was about as subtle as a blast of cannon fire—broadside. At the moment, however, proper social etiquette had a low priority.

"I'm not going anywhere." A slow smile eased across Linc's mouth. "Come sit with me."

She hung back, linking her hands behind her. "What are you doing in town?"

"I've been here since I got back from Pulido."

New pain arced through Erin. He'd been in town all this time and hadn't called or contacted her once. She rocked back and forth on the balls of her feet. Yep, she was better off without him—despite what her heart and body were telling her.

"Well, you chose a good night to drop by. I'd probably be neck deep in water if you hadn't shown up."

His enigmatic gaze holding her, Linc sat up. "I doubt it. You're resourceful enough to have handled the situation on your own."

If she was so resourceful, why couldn't she figure out how to get him to leave before she made a fool of herself and begged him to stay? "Ah, Linc, if there's a point you're leading up to, I'd appreciate it if you'd get to it. It's late, and I want to go to bed."

Wrong words. From the sudden gleam in Linc's eyes, Erin regretted them keenly.

"I want to go to bed, too."

She forced what she devoutly hoped was an innocent smile to her lips. "Well, then, I won't keep you."

Slowly, he uncoiled to his feet. "I want to go to bed with you, Erin."

She backed away. She'd been in this situation before with a hot and bothered Linc. Nothing had ever come of it. Certainly not herself. She refused to—to give in to all the hot and tingly currents of feminine need that presently demanded she launch herself into Linc's arms. Only a dimwit would make the same mistake over and over—

"No comment?" he asked softly, steadily closing the distance between them. "I'd think someone with a mouth as smart as yours would be cutting me down to size about now."

She swallowed. "I'm thinking."

His chuckle was low and seductive. "About how good we're going to be together?"

"What's gotten into you?" Erin demanded, genuinely confused by Linc's sudden turnabout.

He stopped, which was fortunate because one more step would have put them in the same space at the same time. And anyone who knew anything about physics knew—

"*You've* gotten into me, Erin. Into my dreams, into my mind, into my heart. And, rather than go stark, raving mad, I've decided to stop fighting it."

"And what about me and what I've decided?" Pride demanded she bring her hurt feelings into the open. "You deserted me in Mexico, Linc. You walked out on me. Am I supposed to forget that? Am I supposed to forgive that?"

She shook her head, fighting the tears swimming for release. "Because if you expect to drop in and out of my life like some...some studly boomerang, you can just forget it."

"Studly boomerang?" Linc asked incredulously, his dark eyes sparkling. "How do you come up with things like that?"

On the verge of tears, the last thing Erin wanted to do was laugh, or smile, or break the roll she was on. Unfortunately, looking at Linc's tenderly amused expression made her realize how ridiculous her words had been. "You know what I mean."

Linc shook his head. "I started this backward. I should have begun by asking you to marry me and worked my way from there to the bedroom."

"Yes, you should have. You—" Erin broke off as the meaning of his words registered.

"What? No sassy comeback?" he asked, his handsome features oddly vulnerable.

Erin raised her hand to her heart and said the first thing that popped into her head. "You don't have to ask me to marry you to get me to go to bed with you."

Linc swore succinctly, in one syllable. "That's a fine thing to say to a man who wants to spend the rest of his life with you."

"But you don't." She drew in a deep, shaky breath. "I know that."

His hard fingers clamped onto her wrist. "Lord, Erin, I'm sorry for the two times I walked out on you." His grip eased. He stared deeply into her eyes. "But each time I had to leave."

*"Why?"*

The word was torn from the depths of her savaged pride. She knew his answer would determine whether or not she ever trusted him again, whether or not she ever let him make love to her, whether or not she would accept his marriage proposal. So much to hang on one answer. But that answer mattered more than the love or the passion she felt for him.

"Why, Linc? Why did you have to leave?"

"Because I loved you, dammit. Because I wanted to be inside of you more than I wanted to breathe my next breath of air. Because I would have killed to have you."

Gladness and confusion warred within her. "I don't understand. If you felt that way, then why did you leave?"

"Ask me *when,* Erin. Ask me when I first fantasized about stripping away your clothes and taking you to bed."

She licked her suddenly dry lips.

His tortured gaze followed the movement, and he groaned.

"W-when?" she breathed.

"The first time I laid eyes on you. The first time I heard you laugh. Or, more precisely, the first time I saw you laugh at something Merrill had whispered into your ear. I didn't realize it then but I was already jealous of him. Jealous that he'd found you."

Shocked by Linc's confession, by the fury and self contempt lacing his words, Erin fought the urge to recoil, yet she knew intuitively that if she drew back now, she might lose Linc forever. No matter how overwhelmed she might be, she wouldn't risk that, couldn't risk that. They stood at a crossroads, she and Linc. Tonight they would either separate once and for all or they would... She could scarcely shape the thought.

Gently, carefully, Erin touched Linc's cheek. "I never suspected."

Beneath her fingertips, she felt him shudder. His eyes closed. "I made it a point for no one to know or guess."

In that moment, Erin thought her heart would burst from its sudden fullness. Such an honorable man... Such a loyal friend. Her friend. He had proven his friendship in the most challenging way a man could—by denying his own wants and needs. Ultimately, he had been her friend, not Merrill's, and Linc had kept this secret all these years because his own rigid code of honor had demanded it.

"Oh, Linc..."

"That's not all of it," he said hoarsely.

Because Erin sensed his pain as her own, she knew he struggled with yet another burden. She wanted to help him, wanted to banish whatever demons rode him. Drawing upon a hidden well of womanly understanding, Erin wrapped her arms around his waist and hugged him to her. She might not know the words, but with her body she could let Linc know that nothing he could say would push her away.

"I came to despise Merrill. I wanted him out of the picture so I could have you. I moved to Los Angeles because I knew if I stayed, I would... I would tell you how I felt, maybe even seduce you. I thought of seducing you a lot.''

Erin curled herself against his chest. ''I was so unhappy with Merrill, I probably wouldn't have been that difficult to seduce. I didn't make him very happy, Linc. I...I think I'm better at being a mother than a wife.''

Linc's arms closed around her. ''He was a fool, Erin.''

They stood together in silence for several moments. Erin reveled in Linc's power, free at last to accept his strength without fearing being overwhelmed by it.

''I love you, Erin. I want to marry you. I want to have the right to take you to bed and make love with you all through the night.''

Erin closed her eyes. The words she'd ached to hear but hadn't allowed herself to dream of hearing filled her with joy. ''I—I love you, too, Linc. And...and I want the rest of it.''

With his forefinger pressed lightly beneath her chin, he tipped her face toward him. ''The rest?''

''The making love all through the night part. I want that. I don't think I can bear to spend another night alone, wanting you and not having you.''

His head lowered. ''For the rest of my life, I'll take care of you, Erin.''

She understood Linc well enough now to know that for him and the code of honor that governed his actions, he could pledge his love in no other way.

She leaned into the kiss, her heart and her soul meshing to the man. Tears of happiness washed down her cheeks. She had thought she'd found love once. She'd been wrong. With Linc's arms around her,

Linc's tongue wooing her, Linc's hard heat embracing her, Erin knew she'd found the real thing once and for all.

A loud pounding at the front door and male teenage voices yelling "trick or treat" forced them to draw apart.

"Damn, we should have turned off the lights." Linc strode to the front door and ripped it open. He eyed three overgrown boys toting bulging pillow-cases. Linc picked up the orange bucket with what candy was left in it and thrust it at one of the boys. "Here. Go away."

With that Linc closed and locked the door, flicked off the porch light, then moved purposefully toward the lamps. In quick succession, he turned them off. Darkness descended.

"Now where were we?"

He didn't seem to have a bit of trouble locating her in the dark, for he immediately brushed up against her. Erin's fingers found his tie. She gave it a gentle tug. "We were at the good part."

Linc's low laugh made her tingle all over. "That's the only thing I never guessed about you in the years I loved you, honey."

"What's that?" she asked, struggling with the tie.

"That you have a wild streak."

Her soft spurt of surprised laughter caught Erin by surprise. *"What?"*

"A wild streak," he repeated. Then evidently becoming impatient with her clumsy efforts to remove his tie, he relieved her of the task.

Linc's mouth touched the sensitive side of her throat. "Only when you're holding me," she said on a sudden intake of breath. Hot shafts of pleasure played havoc with her insides. "Only when you're holding me..."

"Then I'll hold you for a lifetime."

His words were a pledge and a promise that filled her with hope. Erin knew she would remember this night for the rest of her life, for on this night her life had truly begun. On this night she and Linc had found the courage to claim the love and the passion that had been waiting for them all along.

That they should complete their odyssey on Halloween seemed strangely fitting. After all, both had learned long ago that life had its generous measure of tricks—and treats.

# *Epilogue*

"José, wait up," Joshua called.

Erin looked up from the tomato plant whose ripe, red fruit she was picking and shaded her eyes against the sun. Josh, his legs churning, ran to keep up with the Mexican boy and his dog.

This was Joshua's second trip to Pulido within the last year and, as on his first visit, her son was having the time of his life. The trips had not only given Josh the opportunity to see his grandparents but also provided him with the opportunity to widen his very young horizons. He had even picked up some Spanish, as well as making lots of new friends.

Their visits to Pulido had been good for all of them.

When a pair of darkly tanned arms closed around Erin, she leaned back trustingly against the strong chest she knew would support her.

"You're working too hard, honey."

"No, I'm not."

His wide hands cupped her ripening midsection. "Our baby probably would like a siesta, don't you think?"

Linc's mouth strung warm kisses along her throat. Erin sighed and snuggled against him. "I don't know about baby, but mother could be talked into it."

"Let's cool off at the waterfall first."

A languorous heat spread through Erin. These days, with just a word or touch from her husband, she was ready to make love.

Erin turned in Linc's embrace. The open collar of his khaki shirt allowed her a satisfying glimpse of softly furred chest. She counted the absence of Linc's once obligatory tie a major victory.

"Why are you smiling?" he asked huskily.

She stared into his rugged features. "Because I'm so happy."

"Me, too, darling. This past year has been the happiest of my life."

They stood gazing at each other. For both, the past twelve months had been a time of loving and healing. Josh had thrived within that loving circle and formed a strong bond with Linc. When they returned to Salt Lake City, they would move into the beautiful new home Steve had designed and Prestige Builders had constructed for them.

Linc had brought them to Pulido to donate building materials and expertise to the needy villagers and to give something to the world that had given them so much.

Their hands joined and without speaking they walked toward the river. Erin hadn't accepted the job at the craft shop, after all. Her life had become too crowded with other, more meaningful pursuits, like being Linc's wife and adding to their family.

When they reached the secluded cove that shielded the waterfall, Erin's fingers went to Linc's shirtfront and she began unfastening the buttons.

"You do that so well, darling," he said softly, performing the same task for her.

She pushed his shirt from his shoulders even as the sun warmed her bared breasts. "I've had a good teacher."

His laughter was low, rich and sexy as all get-out. "A labor of love, believe me."

They laid together on the blanket Linc had so cleverly remembered to bring. A few months ago when the miracle within Erin's body had begun to change her appearance, the old tapes had begun to reel through her mind as she had remembered how Merrill had been repelled by her cumbersomeness during pregnancy. Linc's assurances that he still found her beautiful, still found her sexy—along with his impassioned demonstrations—had given her the confidence she needed to let him see her naked.

"I love you, Erin."

"I love you, Linc."

In the next hour Linc proceeded to show her—again—that waterfalls were indeed very romantic places. Later, as she lay within her husband's powerful embrace, the vibrant Mexican sun shone upon her skin. Erin's eyelids drifted shut.

A single thought floated through her mind. Whatever wrong turn she'd taken years ago when she'd married Merrill, she'd corrected it and was now on the right path.

And the path would take her and Linc and Joshua and their unborn child to a lifetime of tomorrows just as wonderful as today had been...

\* \* \* \* \*

# If you've got the time...
# We've got the
# INTIMATE MOMENTS

*Passion. Suspense. Desire. Drama.* Enter a world that's larger than life, where men and women overcome life's greatest odds for the ultimate prize: love. Nonstop excitement is closer than you think...in Silhouette Intimate Moments!

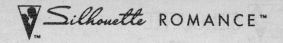
**Silhouette ROMANCE™**

**What's a single dad to do when he needs a wife by next Thursday?**

**Who's a confirmed bachelor to call when he finds a baby on his doorstep?**

**How does a plain Jane in love with her gorgeous boss get him to notice her?**

From classic love stories to romantic comedies to emotional heart tuggers, **Silhouette Romance** offers six irresistible novels every month by some of your favorite authors! Such as…beloved bestsellers **Diana Palmer, Annette Broadrick, Suzanne Carey, Elizabeth August** and **Marie Ferrarella,** to name just a few—and some sure to become favorites!

Fabulous Fathers…Bundles of Joy…Miniseries… Months of blushing brides and convenient weddings… Holiday celebrations… You'll find all this and much more in **Silhouette Romance**—always emotional, always enjoyable, always about love!

# SILHOUETTE®

## *Desire*®

Do you want…

**D**angerously handsome heroes

**E**vocative, everlasting love stories

**S**izzling and tantalizing sensuality

**I**ncredibly sexy miniseries like **MAN OF THE MONTH**

**R**ed-hot romance

**E**nticing entertainment that can't be beat!

You'll find all of this, and much *more* each and every month in **SILHOUETTE DESIRE**. Don't miss these unforgettable love stories by some of romance's hottest authors. Silhouette Desire—where your fantasies will always come true….

### WAYS TO *UNEXPECTEDLY* MEET MR. RIGHT:

♡ Go out with the sexy-sounding stranger your daughter secretly set you up with through a personal ad.

♡ RSVP yes to a wedding invitation—soon it might be your turn to say "I do!"

♡ Receive a marriage proposal by mail— from a man you've never met....

These are just a few of the unexpected ways that written communication leads to love in Silhouette Yours Truly.

Each month, look for two fast-paced, fun and flirtatious Yours Truly novels (with entertaining treats and sneak previews in the back pages) by some of your favorite authors—and some who are sure to become favorites.

### *YOURS TRULY™:*
*Love—when you least expect it!*

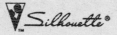

YT-GEN

# SPECIAL EDITION

Stories of love and life, these powerful novels are tales that you can identify with— romances with "something special" added in!

Fall in love with the stories of authors such as **Nora Roberts, Diana Palmer, Ginna Gray** and many more of your special favorites—as well as wonderful new voices!

Special Edition brings you entertainment for the heart!